FAE:
the Fight Against Entitlement

WINGS & WOLF'S BANE

Book Four

Susan Stec & Christopher James Rizzo

Printed in the United States of America

First Edition, November 2023

Cover Design by Susan Stec

Edited by Genevieve Scholl

Formatted by Genevieve Scholl

PROLOGUE

From on top of the silver hills, Rampart watched as the great tree of the Copper Groves clan burned. The latest casualty of the Fae silver war was one of the oldest and strongest holds the revolution had. Ever since the war began, the Erlking's guard had attempted many times to infiltrate the half breed sympathizers without success. But with one large push, their army had finally broken into the city. Rampart and the other rebels fought as hard as they could, but the horde of silver, featureless helmets couldn't be turned back. Eventually, Ozil's call for retreat rang through the battlefield. The destruction of such an important city would be a devastating moral loss to the revolution. One that may turn the course of the war back into the guard's favor.

Rampart clenched his jaw as the fire leapt into the starless night sky. His mind churned, imagining what he could have done different. Would he have been able to help turn back the never-ending tide of Nereus's guard? Probably not. But even with the fresh wound his vision bore into his memory, he knew it was a question that would haunt him the rest of his life. One that could never truly be answered. Rampart wrapped himself in his leathery wings. As a half fae, half imp, there were few cities that would house him in his youth. But the Copper Groves clan took him in, and only asked him to promise to help protect the city if it was in need. A promise he felt lay broken at his feet.

Black blood trickled down Rampart's chin. His fingers traced a sizable cut running the length of his brow. When had he gotten that? His recollection of the battle was nothing more than a collage of steel and magic. Rampart looked for more wounds and found a gash taken out of his wing. Touching it caused a sting of pain, which sparked a memory; the guard dragging away an unconscious Ozil. Rampart tried desperately to save his captain. However, the swarm of soldiers was too much. There was an impact on his wing he hadn't registered before, but now realized was a sword tearing through his flesh.

Rampart bowed his head. Ozil was one of the first fae to see past Rampart's heritage. He taught him how to fight, and even promoted him to ranks no other half fae had reached. Ozil was more than a captain to him; he was a friend and brother. Rampart's mind danced with horrible fates that could befall upon the man he'd followed for so long now that the Erlking had him in his clutches. Two years ago, Ozil was one of the first fae to stand up to Erlking Nereus in his campaign against the half fae. Defying orders, Ozil had turned away from Nereus instead of slaughtering the innocent whose only crime was being born. If he had followed his king's orders, this conflict would have been over before it began, and the Erlking would remain uncontested for the throne.

His refusal led to Nereus's illegitimate daughter, Coralina, leading the half fae against him. Since then, Nereus had felt his stranglehold over the lands loosen. More and more cities answered the call for rebellion and slipped between his weakened fingers. In his desperation, he bore all his cruelty upon his people, continuing his reign by inducing fear amongst them. Fear of what the rebellion could lead to, as well as fear of what would befall his enemies.

Now that Ozil was in his grasp, it was likely he would be made an example of, to persuade others from following his path. Rampart knew it was likely he would never see his friend again, but he wasn't willing to admit that yet. Today's losses were too much already, and giving up that last glimmer of hope felt like snuffing out the last candle of a dark room. For now, he would hold on to the belief of rescue, even if it was just a sweet lie to get him through the night.

Rampart huddled into a ball on the forest floor, wrapped in his wings. His feet would carry him no further, and it was unlikely the guard would think to look for anyone this far from the battlefield. This would be a safe place to rest for tonight, and tomorrow when the battle was no longer fresh, he could continue onward to find Coralina. She would have a plan; he was sure of it. If not, the rebellion could be heading into its darkest days. One way or another, this conflict couldn't continue much longer. There hadn't been such loss of life since the war with the jinn, and the fae were still recovering from that conflict. Rampart could only hope the rest of his people would see their race was in its death throes, and their only chance would be to turn against their old ways of thinking and embrace the changes the half fae could bring.

But fear was a powerful weapon, and Nereus wielded it better than anyone.

CHAPTER ONE

The First Day of a Turn in Events

The Erlking paced the cobblestone of his bedchambers, the rock beneath his feet as cold as his heart. His battle was finely over. Nereus's guard had pushed the half fae from their burning cities and into the Bad Lands. He would be lying if he said the satisfaction would have been greater had there been thousands of heads hung on poles lining the North battlement wall for his viewing pleasure. Instead, there was a meager two hundred and four impaled for the full bloods to see. Yet, the view had diminished even for him as the two hundred and four were now nothing more than skull and bone covered with scraps of clothes that once held the flesh the crows had long ago feasted on. But still, this was Nereus's respite, his reward. That, and the knowledge that any fae that had ventured into the dense and dark woods of the Bad Lands had never returned.

Three months ago, Nereus had ordered all full blooded fae to relocate on the grounds around his castle. From the wooden platforms in the map room and in his private study adjoining his bedchambers, the Erlking was able to watch the development of his people building new cities. With his ban on magicked sunlight in each settlement he destroyed, there was only moonlight and lanterns for the scavengers to forage in the new cities. The mark on his cheek throbbed with his thoughts, a less painful reminder to press on to a new Faery Lands of pure fae. He would finally put an end to the tainted filth in *his* realm.

Nereus climbed the wooden stairs in the room adjacent to his bedchambers and walked the creaky platform from arrowslit to arrowslit viewing the progress of his people.

"Yes! I've driven the half breeds to the Bad Lands," he screamed. "But hear me!" He looked down at his guard training new recruits far below. The fear in their eyes did not register. "If any survive, I'll shove a pole up their arses and out their mouths." Head reared back, he laughed. "I'll hang them in my garden of filth with the others, a constant warning to keep our lands clean."

The imprint on his cheek brought him to his knees with a scream of pain. "Damn you, Calastair! I am not finished with you. May the gods of the damned curse you for your curse on me."

The angel, Calastair, was given the title of Watcher. His words the day he'd cursed Nereus pierced the Erlking's mind. *You don't understand holy fire, do you? It only burns those with wickedness in their souls, and the more there is, the hotter it burns. That wound will never go away either, no magic can heal it, and no glamour can hide it. No matter what you do or what form you take, everyone will be able to see the glow of holy fire on your cheek. And it will continue to burn until you repent and cleanse your soul.*

"Ugh!" The Erlking bent from the pain. "Ahhh!" His hands crushed his temples and ears as Calastair's last words rung loud in the throbbing pain between his palms. *Something tells me, though, you'll be stuck with that mark for a long, long time.*

Nereus climbed to his feet and staggered down the wooden stairs to the cobblestones below. He shook a fist at the moonlit clouds outside the arrowslit. "You are not an angel! You are not a fae! You're a halfblooded monstrosity, Calastair. How dare you curse me!"

Although Nereus had not seen or heard from the Watcher in months, a mental image of his face still haunted the Erlking. Smooth skin, fair, not a blemish on his cocky face. Deep green eyes under fire charged hair. *UGH!*

"An angel with flaming red hair. I hate the atrocity. Someday! Someday I will destroy you."

Nereus cringed under the pain that could have been much worse had he actually committed the threat he screamed into the night. Each time he ordered the demise of another half breed encampment it was almost unbearable, and even more so when he remembered how the slightest thought of cruelty aroused him, joyously.

There was a knock at the door, and Nereus swiftly pulled a mask over his face. He had commissioned a tailor to design it for him to cover the Watcher's curse. It was black leather and worn over half his head and under his chin, leaving eye and ear holes. The day it was delivered, Nereus had the fae put it on him in his bathing room in front of the only mirror in the castle. "It is a beautiful piece of work. I thank you for your service," he had said, and then told the fae, a father of three, "I appreciate your loyalty in keeping your intimate knowledge of my weakness a secret. Although, should you betray me, don't worry, you and your family's deaths will be swift."

A second knock on his bedchamber door, louder and more aggressive, pulled his thoughts from the loyal fae. The Erlking ran his hands over the mask to be sure it was carefully placed. A third knock on the door had Nereus holding a growl behind gritting teeth. "Enter, you fool, before I have your head for the rude disturbance!"

His Regent, Fairl Downs, stepped meekly into the chamber and bowed. "Your Highness, Efrian is here to see you. Shall I send him in?"

"No!" Nereus answered. "Send him to the map room and tell him I will join him shortly."

"As you say." Fairl bowed and backed his way out of the room.

Since his longtime head guardsmen, Ozil, turned on him the day the Watcher had marked him, it was hard for Nereus to trust anyone. But Efrian had slowly proven himself. When Nereus had promised the guard the honor of killing Ozil, Efrian's facial expression did not waver. Still, the Erlking's knowledge of Ozil's whereabouts would remain in a dark and well-hidden cell below the castle.

"Maybe I will make a visit to Queen Reka today," Nereus said, followed by his dreadful chortle. "I need a soothing distraction."

Reka was definitely not *his* queen. In fact, she wasn't a queen at all. Reka was the beautiful fae imprisoned in a beehive by the portal that let the Watcher into his realm. They had a history, he and his queen bee. And after assisting revolutionaries, her new punishment was no visitors. She had only his magicked wasp drones that now guarded every portal coming into his realm as well as her hive.

Nereus left his chambers, his manic whistle heard down the halls of his castle as his bare feet slapped their way to the map room. The habitants of the castle had long since been used to his manic actions. If he wasn't screaming profanities, he was whistling or singing feverishly about the castle at all hours of the day and night.

***

Miles away, weeks after the fire caused the Copper Groves' destruction, a small caravan of fae in wagons formed a circle on the dusty and dry grounds of the Bad Lands. They had pilfered the wagons from abandoned or destroyed villages. It had taken magic to get the nomad wagons over the fence and into the Bad Lands. It was then difficult to keep the animals pulling them safe while navigating in thick woods full of creatures in desperate need of sustenance to survive. Magic attracted them. It was a dismal land where darkness and tension dwelled. Food options were minimal and water tainted. Rampart, accompanied by others, went back over the magicked fence daily to search for supplies. The distance needed to rummage and get back to distribute with success would someday run out. There were still small clans of full bloods, supporters of the Erlking, scattered about the lands. It was a risky endeavor.

The small circle of eight trailers stopped and the dust settled. With the death of so many half fae already, those still fighting to survive out of Faery Lands took to foot and kept on the move for fear of being spotted.

Coralina, a full-blooded air fae jumped down from one of the trailers and ordered they keep magicked light and fire at a minimum while hiding the animals that pulled the trailers.

Coralina was tall, slender, with beautiful blue eyes and a strong and aggressive nature. She was the Erlking's illegitimate daughter, and next in line for the throne, as much his nemesis as he was hers. The difference between the two was Coralina's love for her people. All fae, not just full blooded. She had been the first leader in the revolution, but now shared that billing with Rampart, a half breed. He was strong-minded but a good fighter, having been part of the Erlking's guard. The relationship between the two was fire and ice but equally dutiful. Coralina was good at giving the annoyance he often showed toward her right back at him, frequently.

Rampart rode out of the woods on a black hellhound he called Dusk, equally as annoying as the rider to Coralina because the animal could speak, and not only when spoken to.

As the animal slid to a stop inches from Coralina's leather clad feet, dark, dry dirt wafted over her shoes, legs, and chest, inches from her nostrils.

Rampart slid off Dusk, smiled, and handed Coralina a huge sack. "Turnips," he said, "so play nice with Dusk. He sniffed them out, and we're both hungry as hell."

"That I am," Dusk said in a throaty voice. "It's meat I want, so be nice like my master suggests or I just might have to take a bite out of your skinny ass. However, you can redeem yourself if you give me a little smile and a scratch behind the ear, Coralina."

"I don't do smiles, mutt," Coralina said. "And I'd just as soon skin you and eat you than scratch your mangy fur. You'll eat what we eat, turnips. Remember that when you're sniffing for dinner next time."

The hell hound shook from maw to tail, shedding a mixture of dust, hair, and saliva. "Yeah, no," the animal said. "I don't do turnips. It's dog eat dog in these woods. Here I am, protecting your ass, and what do I get? Turnips. I'll try real hard not to eat one of the fleshy animals in your caravan."

"You do and you'll find yourself pulling a wagon," Coralina said, "or better yet, hogtied over a pit of fire, roasting for tomorrow night's dinner." A corner of the fae's lip went from menacing to a slight upward curve.

With a snort, Dusk turned to Rampart. "We passed a dirty pond close by. I'm going to bathe and quench my thirst before things go bloody here." Dusk raised his brow in Coralina's direction and off the hellhound went, kicking up dry earth in its path.

"Tell me again why you gave that hell of a hound a voice?" Coralina asked as she spit and dusted dirt off her clothing. "He'd be enough of a pain without it."

"He's loyal, and a good weapon," Rampart said. "You are half of the problem. If you left him alone—"

"I've had enough!" Coralina said.

"I, too, but not with my hellhound," Rampart said, his eyes dark and weary. "The capture of Ozil haunts me. I can't live like this. Since the Copper Grove fires all we've done is forage, hide, and try to survive in this horrid place."

Coralina's chest rose and fell. "I'd say that's quite an accomplishment since we're still alive in the Bad lands."

"It's not enough!" Rampart said, and gripped the handle of his weapon tucked in a leather scabbard. "There are hundreds of us. It's time to group, train, and plan an attack that will bring Nereus to his knees. I'm tired of watching broken hearted and disappointed families try to search for a new life. There will be no new life here, only death for all of us. It's time for war, Cora! You need to take your rightful place on the throne. They deserve that."

Rampart was the only person Coralina allowed to use her mother's nickname for her. It had felt too committed, too involved and personal at first, but when he wouldn't quit, she stopped trying. She told herself she had to choose her battles but soon became fond of this one when Rampart only used her full name in uncontrollable disputes. She looked forward to those times as well. "We've tried this, and you know how all of our attempts have gone."

"No. We've only made half-assed attempts that led us right back here. It's time to claim our realm, not defend it." Rampart huffed his frustration, nostrils flaring. "They have never worked to find the powers they possess as half breeds."

"That's because most of our people are working class, not fighters."

"Yes, I admit, Ozil taught me well," Rampart said, his eyes moving to the ground below his boots. "All I'm saying is it's possible. The alternative is death, many deaths, and the certainty is distinction." He looked up. Coralina's gaze was facing off in the distance toward the Castle.

"Look at me," Rampart softly said. "Do you want to spend the rest of your life here in a place that wreaks of death, and magic isn't a tool or weapon, but a beacon to the wretched creatures that now survive by hunting a much easier pray? Us."

Rampart moved his gaze in the direction of Coralina's stubborn eyes. His silver hair fell around his face as he tilted it downward in defeat. His chest was bare, feet too. He fidgeted with the long leather of his scabbard tied around the waist of his leather trousers. His leather-like wings lay on his back, as silver as his hair.

By the sudden glint in Coralina's eyes, she had noticed every movement the Erlking's banished guardsmen made. She placed her hand on Rampart's shoulder.

Rampart turned his head, eyes glassy but jaw set. "Will this ever end? If you won't agree, I will, at the very least, try to save Ozil and together we will attempt to kill Nereus for you and the others."

Coralina replaced sadness with a challenging smile. "I hate when you're right. Let's wait on the rescue of Ozil. The untapped powers of the half breeds could be what saves him, and us."

"We'll begin with those we have here." Rampart's eyes glistened with a hope Coralina hadn't seen in months. "We'll place them in groups of likeness, air, wind, fire, earth, and the pure fae that crossbred among other fae clans. I'll send Dusk to round up the others. It may take a while to get us all together and trained properly, but we will survive."

"Oh, Dusk is going to love that job!" Coralina's eyes sparkled mischievously.

"You are a piece of work," Rampart asked.

Neither held back a much-needed grin.

CHAPTER TWO

Strange Bedfellows

"Again!" Coralina barked over the huffing and puffing of her troops. Twenty half fae lined the convoy of wagons and doubled over in exhaustion.

"Come on, Coralina," a blue haired half gargoyle named Broka said, thick drool dropping off pointy teeth and down his angled chin. "You've been telling us to run laps around the caravan, do jumping jacks, pull ups, basically everything you can think of for an hour now. Give us a break."

Coralina put her hands on her hips and leaned over to be on his eye level. "Oh, I wasn't aware gargoyles gave up so easily. I don't hear the pixie complaining."

"Because... I can't... breathe," said a pink half pixie named Aoife with shiny glittering skin. Her body was small even by fae standards.

"Just give us ten minutes," Broka pleaded. "We rest, then we can do more."

Coralina shook her head. "You're missing the point; you're supposed to be exhausted. We're trying to figure out how to trigger your other half's powers. Meditation didn't work, now we're checking to see if stress and adrenaline can unlock it." She clapped her hands. "Now let's go; everyone on your feet."

The group of half fae grunted and groaned but stood up. All but Broka, who sat down cross legged, green iridescent wings limp on his back. "What is the point?" he said.

Coralina shot him a dirty look. The half gargoyle had been a part of the revolt from the beginning and was one of the more powerful magic users. He was also one of the whiniest. A trait that tended to poke at Coralina's nerves more than any others. "We've been over this, Broka," she said. "If we can combine your fae power with your other half it could unlock new powers to use against the guard."

"That is not what I mean." Broka's head drooped. "The Copper Groves burned; Captain Ozil is captured. Some full blood fae still support us, but most fear the Erlking. At what point do we say we are beaten and look for a way out of the Faery Lands?"

A murmur rippled through the rest of the group in hushed tones as the half fae switched their gaze between him and Coralina.

Broka snapped his head up. His furrowed brow made his pointy cheek bones stand out more than normal. "You all think it; I'll say it! We are losing, and even if we do unlock these powers, there is little hope they will turn this war in our favor. Maybe it is time we figure out an escape option. At least try to save those we can."

The others fell silent, but their eyes carried the same defeated tone as Broka's words. It was a feeling Coralina knew well. There were many times over the last few years those same thoughts had haunted her mind. Combating the guard felt like small waves trying to erode a mountain. But with every defeat, new allies emerged, and with every victory, the sense of hope would return. However, even Coralina had to admit, this was the lowest point the rebellion had experienced.

Coralina clenched her teeth and locked her cold blue eyes on Broka. In a swift motion, she swooped down and lifted him up by his ragged clothing, pinning him against the side of the traveling trailer. "You dumb ass," she snarled. "Where do you think you're going to go to escape Nereus? Now that we've really pissed him off, do you think he won't pursue us wherever we go? And even if somehow we do manage to get away from him, what then? We spend the rest of our lives looking over our shoulders, waiting for one of his assassins to slink out of the shadows?" Coralina turned to the rest of the group. "Look at our caravan; all the half fae brothers and sisters here were spread throughout Faery Lands. Hell, we have entire villages of full blood fae that still support us. Do we have numbers to match the guard? Absolutely not." She stuck her finger in Broka's face. "But those who have been here since the beginning should know we started with a lot less. We'll rebuild and persist. The Erlking can thin us, but he can't crush us. So let's stop all the complaining and get back to being a thorn in his side."

The half fae were still silent, but in the corner of Aoife's mouth, Coralina saw a hint of a smile, and that would have to do. "Now, let's figure out these powers so we can teach the rest of the half fae how to do it," Coralina said. "On your feet, let's go. Two more laps around the caravan. And if adrenaline doesn't unlock anything, we'll try the next theory and then the next till we find out why Nereus and the jinn fear the half fae."

The group nodded and slowly started their jog. Broka hesitated a moment but nodded to Coralina before chasing after the rest. He may be a pain in her butt, but she knew in the end Broka would be loyal to the cause. She just wished he would shut up once and a while.

"Cora!" a voice shouted from behind. Coralina turned to see Rampart running toward her, his footsteps thudding against the soil like a youngling excited to show off his latest find. "I need you in the command tent. There's someone here you should talk to!"

It had been a long time since she had seen him this excited. Seeing his smiling face gave her a warm feeling she couldn't figure out yet. But it gave her hope there was a new ally to their cause waiting for her. "Did Dusk find someone when he was rounding up the other half fae?"

"No, he's still trying to find everyone. Someone else came to us on his own." Rampart stopped a few inches from her. "This could be big for us, maybe even game changing."

Coralina's eyes sparked. Rampart wasn't the type to exaggerate. It made her mind dance with possibilities. "Okay, so who..."

"Come on, I'll show you." Rampart swung around and quickly walked toward the command center.

"Hey, can't you just... ugh!" Coralina chased after him. "This better be good," she said, glancing back at the half fae." If I'm not there to push them, we'll probably come back to a cluster snooze."

"Don't worry, you can get back to torturing Broka soon enough," Rampart said with a laugh. "But this is important." When he reached the tent made from particle leaves, Rampart spun on his heal to face Coralina. The abrupt move almost sent them tumbling to the ground. "Now, I will tell you, it's important to keep an open mind."

She smiled. "You calling me close minded, Ramp?" Her expression dropped. *Ramp? Have I ever called him that before? Why did I have to be strange and blurt that out?*

If Rampart noticed, he didn't say anything. "No, but I know you, and I'm worried when you see him you may have a knee jerk reaction. Just promise me you'll hear him out."

Coralina frowned. "Rampart, who is in there?"

Rampart hesitated. "His name is Aldul. He's here as a representative of the jinn."

Coralina's eyes narrowed as her emotions bounced from surprise to anger. She waited for Rampart to crack a smile and say it was just one of his off-kilter jokes, but his gaze remained firm and serious. "You brought a jinn into this camp," she growled through clenched teeth, checking over her shoulders to make sure no one was in ear shot range. "Are you out of you mind?!"

Coralina pushed him aside and slid through a twig woven door. The room held several chairs made from hollowed out acorns and a table with a crudely drawn map. On the other side stood the jinn in his smokey form, his white eyes glowing through billowing green and gold clouds.

"Get out!" she yelled at the hazy figure. "How dare you come here!"

Rampart hurried after her. "Cora, you promised you'd hear him out."

"I absolutely did not, and what in the river Stix made you think I would? No deal with the jinn has ever led to anything for the fae other than misery and death." She glared back at Aldul. "How did you even get into Faery Lands? No, wait, I don't even care. You have to go now!"

Aldul raised two smoky hands. "I don't want to be a disruption to you or your camp. I'm merely here as a liaison for the jinn in your rebellion."

"We don't need a liaison; haven't you been listening?" Coralina snapped and took a step forward.

A hand from behind grabbed hold of her forearm. Coralina turned to push Rampart off, but his grip was strong. "Please, Coralina," he said with stern eyes. "Just trust me on this one. You're going to want to hear what he has to say." His voice was calm but carried weight.

A chill ran down her spine. It was rare for him to speak like that to her, and when he did it usually meant it was important. Coralina shifted a side eye to Aldul. "Because of the respect I have for Rampart, I'll hear what you have to say. But keep in mind I have many powerful faeries in this camp. You say the wrong thing and I'll have them descend on this room quicker than you can... I don't know... float out of here."

The jinn nodded. "It won't be necessary," he said. "I know you don't have any reason to believe me, given the history between our people, but I promise I'm not here as a threat to you or your camp." Aldul's voice was soft and sounded young.

Coralina finally yanked her arm from Rampart's grasp. The two fae took a seat at the table, though Coralina sat in a way she'd be able to fly up at a moment's notice.

"Thank you," Aldul said, gliding closer to the table. "I've come here to talk to you in person, and I've shrunk to your size so we can speak face to face."

Coralina crossed her legs. "Yes, get down on our level so to speak. Like how a parent gets down on a knee to talk to a small child."

Aldul hesitated. "That was... not the image I wanted to portray. More like I was trying to show you respect in your home." The jinn shook his head. "Let me start again. I'm here because there has been a fundamental change in the jinn's approach to foreign relations. Due to recent events, especially the one's involving Talock, the jinn people have spent time... how to put this, re-evaluating our stances and beliefs."

Coralina snorted. "Yeah, I bet that's been a PR nightmare for you guys, hasn't it?"

Aldul bowed his head. "Indeed. Probably more than you know. Talock and his views represent a period of time many jinn have turned away from. There were many who didn't support the treaty even back when it was signed with your people. But we were seduced with promises of peace, and assurance our people would thrive under it." Aldul sighed. "However, we now see it as a black mark on our history, especially after the crimes Talock has committed recently. The jinn people have a desire to distance themselves from reminders of the past, and especially, with laws that were signed under Talock's name."

Coralina leaned forward. "What are you saying?"

"I'm saying our leaders no longer wish to hold the fae to the restrictions put forth on the treaty signed between Talock and Nereus. That the jinn people no longer wish to restrict who the fae are allowed to breed with, and that Faery Lands will no longer be held under our thumbs."

The feeling in Coralina's legs numbed. She looked at Rampart with a slack jaw. He sat there beaming his 'told you so' face that normally irritated her to no end, but this time she welcomed. If what Aldul was saying was true, it could be a monumental shift in Faery Lands. The main argument Nereus used to justify the ban on interspecies breeding was the threat of jinn retaliation. If that was removed, it would be a major blow to the Erlking's supporters. Her heart fluttered with the possibilities that could unlock for the rebels but did her best not to show it.

Coralina stood to meet Aldul eye to eye. "If that's true, why are you here? Shouldn't you be talking to Nereus?"

"That is a discussion that will take place, of course. However, many of us believe he will not be supportive of our decision. And of his own accord, will keep the ban instituted." Aldul crossed his arms. "That puts us in an uncomfortable situation. On one hand, he is the king of this land and it isn't our place to interfere. On the other, the ban will forever be linked to the jinn people, and as long as it is in effect, will be a stain on our name."

Rampart's eyes dulled. "So, wait, are you saying you won't be able to supply any troops to our cause?"

"I'm afraid not."

Coralina tapped her elbow. "Even if they did offer, I wouldn't be able to accept them. Think about it, my father gained control by using the threat of the jinn. I can't be a symbol of change for our people if I do the same thing."

Rampart nodded. "That's true, I guess."

"Our hope is this will weaken the Erlking's position amongst his people," Aldul said. "If he continues the ban without jinn support, we hope to bring more soldiers to your cause." The green and gold smoke creased into a smile. "And I was also sent here to help your half fae. We know you have been trying to unlock their potential. I might not know exactly how to do this, but I have some theories, and I have been given permission to try and help you figure it out, under the restrictions of not engaging in battle myself."

Rampart tapped Coralina's leg. "So what do you say, happy I didn't throw his ass out?"

CHAPTER THREE

An Act of Need with a Jinn's Speed

Rampart watched Coralina's hips sway as she headed back to her group of trainees. The fae stirred his emotions. Feelings he wished to keep deep and cold, not smolder and rise to the surface. Rampart had once fallen into an abyss of affection motivated by more than a physical attraction. It hadn't ended well. A warrior's heart was not easily pulled from a lifelong ambition to a devoted liaison that limited a combatant's concentration. Together, neither served well enough to be worthy of either.

"I see your fae is not pleased with me," Aldul said from behind. "But I will win her over. I cannot go back to my people before doing so."

Rampart sighed. "She'll get over it the minute she sees you're not only a valuable asset to our cause but the only way to gain motivation and an unconditional dedication from the half breeds." He pulled his eyes off Coralina and turned to face Aldul. "They need to trust you and feel a great respect for you."

"I understand. This will be a difficult task and needs deep thought on my part." The jinn stood and faded until he was a smoky silhouette of green and gold. "I will float in the Gray around the camp tonight, deep in thought, and by tomorrow I hope to come up with a plan. While I love a challenge, Rampart, I also love my realm. I have to meet my leader's expectations."

Aldul's form floated closer to Rampart. "So, do not worry, I will carry out this mission using the best of my abilities." The smokey silhouette wavered as the voice of the jinn added, "And that would be to slide open a curtain on this realm and step into a void called the Gray where only someone like me from Hell, or an angel from Heaven, can enter. There I can roam unseen among those outside of the Gray. I will observe and listen undetected and unheard."

Rampart smiled broadly and stood to address the jinn before the wavering form seeped back into its hiding place. "I have a perfect way for you to accomplish your challenge *before* morning. You want to hear it?"

***

"Bring that family to me. Now!" Nereus shouted. "People! Witness this because you could be next. I will not tolerate insolence, deceit, or any threat to my realm. We are too close to perfection. This family has broken our building codes. No one will have an abode larger than another. We are all equal in Faery Lands. Not even my guardsmen will have bigger and better homes. The only supreme fae is your Erlking!"

A group of guardsmen jumped to attention and turned toward the Erlking, expressions of fear on their faces. They had been part of the group scrutinizing full bred fae building their dwellings in the woods adjacent to the East wing of the castle.

By direct order of the Erlking, full blooded fae came from all over Faery Lands to build new communities surrounding the castle. Shortly following each such order, Nereus had destroyed their towns.

Randomly, the Erlking strolled through the construction of his new villages. And as he did today, ordered random and unjustified deaths. These were not limited to adult fae, but changelings as well. Even guardsmen were not protected. The monthly count hit thirty yesterday when the Erlking had sentenced a young female sprite to a fiery death. He had her wings removed, put her in a cage, and set her afire. The cage was one of several hung from poles in a small section of the graveyard where Nereus had skewered other "tainted" or "disobedient" fae for months. The sprite was damned for posting a willingness in one of the town squares to share her dwelling with another single female sprite just hours ago. Nereus had accused her of unnatural attractions. As they lit the fire under her cage the sprite cried thanks for not causing another's death. No one had answered the post yet.

The victims' levels of pain before their death depended on the crime committed: non-code building, a demon injecting itself into the communities to breed, or simply a half breed pretending to be pure. There was no tolerance for others who tried to prove the Erlking's incorrect judgement. Those that tried were swiftly added to the death toll. Yet some struggled with the unjust deaths and tried to defend family members, friends, or neighbors with the hope their Erlking would understand their plight.

As this accused family was brought forward, a guard moved along side of them. "Sire, please. This family is up to code. I tended to this myself. In addition to this, they have been seen by the castle seer, and she has confirmed their full blood legitimacy. Have mercy. They're dryads from the Western Woodsmen tribe. At birth, the youngest male was prophesized to be a protector like his great grandfather and will serve you well someday."

Nereus adjusted the black leather mask further under his chin. His eyes jerked here and there as if he were searching for answers among the crowd that was forming around the guard and dryad family.

The father stepped forward, the trowel in his hand shaking. He set it down at his feet and wiped his hands on the apron he wore. He dropped to one knee and bowed his head. "Although we've done nothing wrong, take me my Erlking. Let my wife and children make any corrections you see fit—"

"Why would I let any of you live if I believed you were sent by demons from the deepest pits of Hell to destroy me and my people?"

The crowd did not verbally or physically show objections for the swift change in the Erlking's condemnation.

The dryad father did not raise his head. "But, Your Highness, I assure you, this is not true. What test can I take to prove our loyalty?"

"A demon bleeds black!" Nereus said as if speaking to someone not visible to the others. He paced with movements as sporadic as his jerking eyeballs. "I do not have time for this. Behead them all and be done with it! I must heed the light of my visions no matter the pain. The pain is verity!"

Guards pulled the family to the ground. The mother dragged the smallest to her chest, but the faeling was swiftly pulled away. A knife blade caught the sun before it scathed the father's left shoulder to the center of his chest. As the child was forced to his knees, the blade sliced his father's blood into the left side of his son's throat, and in seconds they were both dead. Their mother's screams cut though the complete silence of the crowd around her.

"Shut that demon's screams!" Nereus growled. "Now!"

The blade swung for the last time and the head of the wife and mother rolled across the grass and stopped before the Erlking's feet.

Nereus swung a hand over the butchered family of fae, green grass cradling their lifeless bodies, and then swung his open hand at the crowd. "There is only pain and darkness here!" Nereus fell to his knees. "The pain!" he screamed. "The pain speaks the truth!" The Erlking grabbed for his cheek, eyes closed, and moaned. He swung his hand backward at a guard standing by the cart he'd disembarked from shortly before. "Take me! Now!"

As the Erlking's men moved him onto a stretcher made of woven lemongrass and soothing lavender, the Erlking rolled to his side. The four male fae were bare-chested and muscular with dark hair, tanned skin, and silver eyes. They were fire fae, and powerfully efficient guards. Fire fae wielded strength and strong magic. However, they were not fit for the guard because of their inability to keep their temperament under control and impulsive actions. In the Erlking's case, any attempt on his life was not just well guarded but extremely protected. Nereus had never used them outside of Faery Lands or in his defense with any outside creatures. Their usage brought strong ramifications from the gods governing otherworld creatures.

As fire fae carried the Erlking to the carriage, Nereus pointed at the guardsman who had spoken out. "You! Take all of them to the poles! Or be killed yourself. It is your choice!"

It was clear by the pinched brows, downturned lips, and the pain in the eyes of the guard, the deaths of this family was on his head. But he also knew it could be worse if he did not obey immediately. He felt saddened by his luck as he began to pick up the bodies to take to the Erlking's dark garden.

***

Aldul had taken on more of solid form and sat at the map table in Rampart's hut. "This is a big thing you ask of me."

"Yes, I'm aware of that," Rampart replied. "But it will endear you to half fae and the full blooded. There are many fearful of Nereus, but your aggressive move against him will definitely show your loyalty with our revolutionaries and get their attention. As you said, the fae do not trust the jinn, and most hate them. Our mission, whether successful or not, will change that frame of mind in all fae."

"I feel this to be true," Aldul said, "but I have no authority—"

"You said they expected you to handle your mission," Rampart said. "Alone. You told me they did not give you instruction as to how you gain respect or get the job done. All they expect is results; the end of the treaty and respect from the fae. I can promise you, after we do this, it will end the fear that all jinn are demons and unreliable."

It was a good sell, but still the jinn hesitated. "I would, at the very least, have to get permission from my superior."

"It's too risky," Rampart said. "And it shows no strength to ask after told not to. It needs to be your choice, alone, to show my people you were sent, respected by the jinn, and took the initiative to do the job swiftly with a strength we can also respect."

Aldul rubbed a stubble on a magicked chin on resolidified body. "When will we do this?"

"Tonight after the camp settles down," Rampart said. "We both use the Gray to make us invisible, right?"

"Yes; I can take you inside with me."

"That's why I feel this is the right thing to do. You are a gift sent by the gods." Rampart pulled out the only other chair at the map table and sat.

Aldul laughed. "Imagine, a demon sent to Faery Lands by the gods!"

Rampart's loud and equally amused response ramped up the jinn's comradery.

***

Nereus saw his reflection as he climbed out of lavender bathwater. He had dismissed the fire fae but knew they would be outside his chamber doors all night. That and the warm bath was a welcomed reprise from the day. The handprint on his cheek glowed and pulsed with his heartbeat, but the pain was minimal now. When he had returned to castle, he stood on the platform in the map room and watched the dryad family of six tied to poles in the garden of death at the hands of two of his fire fae. The Watcher's brand had been so painful he lost consciousness, fell to the cement floor, and rolled under the wooden platform. He woke to the smell of lavender in a tub of warm water off his bedchambers. A female fire fae was bathing him. His hand flew to his face. The mask was still in place.

Nereus dismissed the chamber maid with thoughts of his bed and dreams of his accomplishments. Maybe tomorrow he would kill Ozil. The life of the fae was getting more annoying since the decrease of his peoples' mourning for his former head guardsman.

***

Aldul and Rampart stood before a guard sleeping in a kicked-back chair balanced on a wall five feet from the cell that held Ozil. The chamber was dark and damp with only two candles burning on the wall behind the guard and no openings in the walls surrounding them to let in fresh air. Ozil sat bent at the waist, the small of his back against the damp wall, and a pile of straw scattered under him. Odors of urine, excrement, and death mingled foul and fetid.

"Will getting him out of the cell be difficult?" Rampart's voice was a throaty whisper.

Neither the fae sleeping in the chair by the cell, nor the guards they passed in the halls of the castle had any idea that the Erlking's previous lead guard was about to disappear.

"Getting him out and up to Nereus's room will be quite simple while in the Gray," Aldul replied. "The threat will be when we step out and wake the Erlking to tell him why I'm here."

CHAPTER FOUR

Burned Bridges on a Starless Night

Nereus stirred in his bed. Like most nights, the Erlking woke with burning pain on his cheek. A recollection of a dream dissolved. Whatever it was had ignited the holy fire. Nereus grimaced, more from anger than pain. The thought of the angel judging him from afar made his blood boil. And he refused to let it influence his decisions, for doing so would feel like a defeat to him unlike any he had suffered before.

Nereus slipped out from beneath the sheets woven from the softest dogwood seeds his men could find. He sat on the edge of the bed, head hung, while he waited for the pain to pass. The glow from the handprint on his cheek illuminated the room. As he cleared his mind, the light dimmed to the level of candlelight. The pain was still there, but manageable.

In a move that was now routine, Nereus slid out of bed, donned a blue and silver robe, and reached for his leather mask. He would commonly walk the halls of the castle at night till he could attempt sleep once again. But tonight his thoughts drew him somewhere different. He walked barefoot down the cold spiral stairs to the dungeon, where he could talk to his once loyal Captain.

***

Rampart stood in front of the cell of his mentor and friend. Beyond the steel bars Ozil hung, arms chained to the wall. His roach like wings cuffed to his body. Black grime smeared over his cheeks and long pointy ears. Even in such a vulnerable state, the captain still looked strong. His head bowed forward with his bright orange eyes closed, but Rampart didn't sense any break in the fae. In fact, he wouldn't have been surprised if Ozil sprung up from his kneeling position to free himself at any moment.

Aldul stood beside Rampart. Since they were in the Gray, he took his physical form. Green skin with shimmering gold symbols decorating his cheeks and neck. "The cuffs might be a problem," he said. "I don't believe I can phase him into the Gray without taking them, too."

"Hmm." Rampart walked in front of the sleeping guard.

Outside of the Gray, in the bowels of the castle, it was dark and drained of color. Everything appeared as levels of shadow.

"I could try to sneak his keys from him," he said. "I'm sure one of them would open the lock."

"Do you think you could do it without waking him?" Aldul asked. "I'd rather like to avoid turning this into some kind of prison riot."

Rampart laughed. "Actually, that sounds like quite a bit of fun. But, yes, I can be sneaky when I need to be." He pointed to his leathery silver wings. "I do have imp blood coursing through my veins after all."

"Very well. I'll pull back the veil and let you out. I'll keep it open so if there's any sign you are detected you can hop back in."

Rampart nodded and crouched down behind the guard. "Got it. Ready when you are."

Aldul nodded and pulled back the veil. Rampart snuck through. A flickering candle by the guard's desk turned the drab gray brick into dancing shadow light. His nostrils filled with an assortment of feted smells from the damp chamber. With light steps, he moved closer to the guard.

The skeleton keys hung on his belt, their ring attached by a leather strap. With delicate fingers, Rampart unhooked the strap while supporting the keys to keep them from jingling. The guard breathed heavily in his sleep but didn't stir. With a few small steps back, Rampart slipped back into the Gray, and Aldul shut the breach.

"Well done," Aldul said with a smile. "If anything of mine goes missing, I know who I'm questioning first."

Rampart spun the key ring on his index finger. "Sleeping inept guard, kids' stuff." He stepped through the steel bars like they were pillars of smoke. "The real trick is figuring out which one of these ten keys go to the cuffs and getting Ozil into The Gray without making noise." He started flipping through the ring. "Some of these are obviously cell door keys, but there's five smaller keys. Guess we'll just have to pop in there and do a little trial and error." He turned towards his companion, but the jinn's attention was aimed toward the dungeon staircase.

"Hold on," Aldul said. "I think someone is coming."

The two watched as a shadow crept down the stairway wall till the figure of Nereus holding a glow worm lantern came into view. Even within the Gray, the site of the Erlking sent shivers down Rampart's spine. Physically, Nereus wasn't the most imposing figure, but his presence and pose drew fear from his enemies. He might as well been the size of the castle spires.

Nereus glided over to the sleeping guard and peered down with fire in his eyes. He reached down and gently shook the guard's arm. The guard slowly woke and rubbed his eyes; when he looked up and saw who stood over him, he jumped to his feet so fast they hopped off the ground. "I'm sorry, sir," he said with a trembling voice. "I wasn't aware you were coming down to see the prisoner. Is there something I can help you with?"

Nereus's cold eyes bore into the guard's. "Can you help me? I suppose you could. You see, in the cell behind you sits the most notorious traitor of our time. One of the leaders of the rebellious horde that has split our lands and watered our forest with loyal soldiers' blood. So what I would like from the guard I put in charge of keeping this dangerous fae behind bars is, at the very least, to be able to stay conscious while on duty."

The guard shifted nervously. "Of course, sir. I can't explain how sorry I am. It's just, the guy who usually relieves me took ill and I've been down here for... you know what, it doesn't matter, it's no excuse."

"No, it isn't," Nereus said, and waved a hand over a cup the guard had on his desk. Water lifted from the cup and floated at the tip of his index finger. "And I'll look into getting someone to replace you." The water formed a shimmering knife blade and shot from the Erlking's finger. Seconds later, blood spewed from a gash in the guard's neck. With wide eyes, the fae grabbed for his throat and dropped to his knees. Blood ran through his fingers. With burbling gasps, he fell onto the stone floor.

Nereus watched, his one eye glistening, his breath panting excitement. He showed no sign of pain as the glaring light from his mask turned the drab color of the cell floor from gray to a vivid pool of red.

Rampart stood motionless. There had been many times he'd been forced to kill fae soldiers on the battlefield, but it was never something he took lightly. It disgusted him how easily Nereus could turn on those under his rule.

Aldul watched Ozil as the guard studied the Erlking over snarling lips. "You might want to be careful," he muttered through dry cracked lips in a deep gritty voice. "If you keep killing your own men, there won't be anyone to fight for you."

The Erlking smirked. "No worries. We have plenty of fae still loyal to their king." He carefully stepped around the pool of blood growing on the ground. "I do find it amusing you still speak as if the little band of traitors are still a threat to my kingdom. In case you weren't aware, Coralina and what's left of your revolution were last seen running like scared roaches into the bushes."

Ozil chuckled. "As long as Coralina lives, there is still hope."

Nereus shook his head. "After a defeat, there are always little groups left to clean up. But if Coralina ever shows herself again, we'll easily eradicate what's left of your movement."

Rampart clenched his jaw. It was hard for him to stand there and listen to the Erlking's dismissive words. His emotions always were close to the surface. At least in the Gray he didn't have to worry about saying anything stupid.

The veteran Ozil gave no sign he was bothered by Nereus's threats. "Is that why you've come here in the middle of the night? To tell me you're not worried about Coralina anymore? It would seem something has kept you up."

Nereus narrowed his eyes. "I come and go where and when I wish. And that is not your concern anymore, is it?" He clasped his hands behind his back and looked down at the dead guard. "Do you know why this man died? It wasn't just because of his failure at his post, although that would have been enough reason. No; this was an action you've forced me into."

Ozil raised an eyebrow, chuckled, and with a phlegmy voice, said, "Me? Come now, we both know you need no one to force cruelty and sadistic behavior from you."

"You are wrong. You were my right-hand man, the one person I trusted above all others. Together we kept this land in peace, no one dared step out of line, and they trembled as we walked by. Then, you did the unthinkable. You turned from your king when I needed you most. Instead of ending the revolution before it started, you helped spark it." Nereus straightened his back. "It occurred to me, perhaps I put too much trust in you, maybe I had been too lenient on the citizens. This man, and countless others, have perished at the slightest hint of failing me to keep others from following in your footsteps. So that no one would even dare to speak against me or risk the threat of death. All because of you."

Ozil didn't flinch. "Please, you and I know each other too well for me to believe that bullshit. How many times have you told me you felt slighted by the citizens of Faery Lands, and that you thought you deserved their love for the treaty with the jinn, not their ire?" Ozil sneered. "You've wanted to be given an excuse to show your ruthlessness for years, and now you can use the revolt as a reason to punish those that don't give you their undying loyalty."

Ozil shifted and, with effort, clamored to his feet, his arms bent uncomfortably to his sides. "You can't hide it from me. I could see it in your eye when you killed the guard. You get a thrill from putting your boot on the necks of those around you, enemies and allies alike. And this revolution has given you a chance to do it. If I didn't know better, I would say you were enjoying this war. However, I know what hides under that mask." Ozil lowered his voice to a growl. "Tell me, how has that holy fire been judging your actions, Nereus?"

Nereus's jaw clenched. "Sounds like you know everything, do you?" He spat with irritation at the mention of his name instead of his title. "Well, here's something that may be news to you. Tomorrow I'm ordering every citizen in the capital to the town square. They will all celebrate as I announce the end of the revolution, and at the climax of the celebration I will hang you in front of everyone. In one short drop and sudden stop, you will become the sign everyone will remember as the end of the rebellion, and the unwavering strength of their Erlking." Nereus leaned close to the cell bars. "That, is what I wanted to tell you."

The two exchanged hard expressions before Nereus turned and headed back to the stairwell. The lantern light faded as he ascended.

Rampart moved next to Aldul, peeking up the spiral staircase to make sure the Erlking was gone. "Alright," he said, "now that the horrible conversation is over, let's break out the captain before he sends another guard down to replace the one he killed."

CHAPTER FIVE

Philanthropy Trapped in a Gilded Cage

"Look, you are not my master, so get off my back or shut up." Dusk growled as he leapt fallen trees long dead and turned to coal.

"Maybe not," Coralina said, "but right now I have the reins, so I'd appreciate it if you maneuver as I direct before we both end up dead."

"Nothing is going to kill me. I was born here, raised here. Do you want to end up in the right part of Copper Groves? I know where I'm going, do you?"

Coralina gripped a fist full of fur and leaned into Dusk as the hellhound jerked left to avoid a boulder that popped five feet out of the ground in front of them. "I hate this damned place," she said with a hiss.

"Well, I feel right at home."

"Screw you!" Coralina shouted as Dusk dropped to the ground and slid under a snarled nest of charred nettle. The stinging hairs of the plant scrapped her wings and hair but saved her skin from a pain she would have dealt with later if she hadn't tucked her legs and arms under her body and buried her face in the hellhound's fur.

The Bad Lands were the underbelly of Faery Lands, an inverse, a transcendent and curious novelty. Although everything was not dead in this wretched place, it looked dead. It was dark and dreary, void of color with only shades of death. The creatures that took refuge here were mythical nightmares, handed down for generations: Aswang, a shape shifting creature that eats newborns. Grootslang; snakes as large as an elephant. Wendigo; cannibalistic monsters. La Ciguapa with backward feet; enchanting women that lure men into the woods. Bunyip: grotesque water spirits that lurk in swamps and creeks, hungry for human flesh. Harpy, guardians of Hades, a creature with the head of a woman, agents of torturing punishments.

And there were many others, including the Hellhound. Dusk's kind were fiery-eyed creatures as black as the Bad Lands and carried within them a guardian, a servant of hell or the underworld.

Dusk crawled out the other side of the nettle bush and stood next to the fence that would take them out of the Bad Lands and into Faery Lands.

Coralina sat up straight on the Hellhound's back, her piercing blue eyes threatening. "Who the hell controls you, you thick-headed pain in my ass?"

"Remind me to bag some of that nettle on the way back." Dusk looked over his shoulder at Coralina with calculating attention. "You can boil up a tea. It will give your trainees energy."

"Don't change the subject. What do you carry inside your soul, Hellhound?"

"You know, Rampart asks me that at least once a month," Dusk said, and without warning, the hellhound reared back and jumped the fence.

"And how do you answer him?" Coralina said through gritted teeth, then jumped off the hound's back. She spread her wings, giving them a flutter. White hair with the smallest hint of yellow tint fell over her shoulders and bounced around on her juddering wings.

"I don't," Dusk said.

"UGH! You're a horrid creature."

"Indeed. Isn't it grand?" Dusk shook from head to tail until his black hair stood on edge. He looked down with flaming red eyes locked on her icy blue ones.

"I will never ride you again!" Coralina spat.

"Never say never." The corners of the hellhound's maw turned up in a grin. "Hop on unless you want me to leave your faery white ass right here and let you hike it back to camp empty handed."

Coralina's chest rose and fell. Her nostrils flared with noisy contempt. "I hope there are enough rations left in Copper Groves to fill the sacks we brought." Her mood was clear with each forced word. "We need fresh water and food. Lots of food. Magicked rations from dry timber in this hellhole look good, but they won't keep us alive."

Dusk snorted a laugh. "You actually tried to serve the fae magicked, charred and foul, eatables only a hound from hell could appreciate with its last dying breath?" The creature shook its head. "You are a real piece of work."

"No, you idiot. I made a joke instead of kicking you in the ass."

Dusk snorted. "Next time, kick me. I'd understand that. We hellhounds are very literal creatures with an impulsive short fuse. Say what you mean. It could save your life." Dusk lowered his hind end and bumped Coralina's shoulder with his rump. "Hop on; I'd like to get back before Rampart and the jinn."

***

"Being in the Gray is interesting," Rampart said, "but still, I find it hard to believe the Erlking can't drum up enough magic to see, or at least sense us, before we confront him."

"He cannot ... well, unless a jinn or angel assists him. And with Talock under lock and key, I doubt he could find a willing subject." Aldul smiled. "However, should he have either at the moment, they would have been banned from heaven or hell, and therefore, not easily able to draw extra power from our realm, like myself. Besides, the great Allah would not allow this. He created us from smokeless fire the day after he created humans. Humans are Allah's hope, angels are the army of Allah, and jinn are fire and nightmare and must be watched. But we do not meddle with the unworthy. Allah himself takes care of their outcome. Talock is a good example."

"And what about a crazy ass fae like me?" Ozil asked.

Aldul laughed. "Fae, my friend, are from the realm of enchantment. There is no definitive way, earthly or unearthly, to handle an issue of magic apart from being in the middle of it. Which is exactly where we are located at the moment."

"And we're here to save your crazy ass," Rampart said over a chuckle.

"Oh good." Ozil grunted as he tried to get his feet under him. "I thought you were just visiting. Get me the hell out of here."

"In due time," Adult said. "My reason for being here is to confront Nereus, but as long as we're here..." The jinn chuckled.

"I'm here if you need me," Ozil said. "Not myself, but still capable."

"You will remain in the Gray," Rampart warned.

"The hell I will," Ozil grunted as he hobbled toward them.

Rampart and Aldul each lifted one of Ozil's arms around their shoulders. There was a long stairway ahead that lead up to the Erlking and Queen Mabyn's chambers, and Ozil was clearly not himself.

"I will not apologize for expecting the worst when we confront Nereus, Aldul," Rampart said, and turned to Ozil, "but, Captain, I will die trying to save and serve you again. So, for the moment, don't do anything you know you—"

"—can't do. I get it, Rampart." He turned to Aldul. "I have no idea why you are here, Jinn, but I thank you for making me part of it. However, in the end, Aldul, the fae will find a way to end this Erlking's reign. With or without the power of the Gray."

"Hear me, both of you," Aldul said. "My body is strong; my abilities are stronger. The Gray is where I can do the most damage, but be assured, you are safe with me in or out of the Gray."

"My magic is strong, too," Ozil said, "but like any creature, I have limitations and that's what allowed the Erlking to capture and hold me. I believe all creatures to be the same."

"This is true, Chief Ozil," Aldul said, "but do you think my people would send any jinn to confront the Erlking of a fae world?"

"No. Even I wouldn't have held someone high enough unless I was absolutely sure they could do the job." Ozil tightened his arm around Rampart. "I knew when I met Rampart he was destined for big things. And here he is, doing what I thought impossible, and making me proud of my perception."

Rampart grinned. "Let's save that kind of talk for when we get you safely to the Bad Lands."

"The Bad Lands?!" Ozil stopped several steps from the top of the rock stairway and removed his arms from their shoulders. "I can't believe you've made a home in the pit of hell and are here to tell me about it."

"And he lives quite comfortably with many others under his command." Aldul laughed loudly. "We will get you there safe and sound so you can see for yourself."

Ozil jerked his head upward and pressed himself flat against the wall as two guards turned the corner and headed down the stairs.

Aldul's laughter became even louder. "They cannot hear or see us. I told you this. You both look like a hunter's mounted prize."

"I feel like a hunter's prize," Rampart said.

Ozil's eyes were wide and so was his mouth as he watched the faeries' descent.

When the guards passed, Aldul said, "None the less, we should move swiftly. They may be on their way to the dungeons."

Rampart put his arm around Ozil again. "Yes. The sight of an abandoned cell is sure to stir up a good deal of frenzied action."

As the three climbed the last five steps, Ozil spoke to Aldul. "My guard and I could conquer many a confrontation with the ability to surprise and a place to retreat. Would it be too much to ask that you be at our service in the future?"

As the two fae and the jinn walked down the hall and into the upstairs chambers, Aldul replied, "I wish it were so, my friend, but it is not. As with all creatures, there are great penalties for misusing the powers Allah gave us. Though it is hard to kill or capture a jinn, Talock, the jinn that started this war, *was* captured *and* imprisoned by the Otherworld Council. He has lost all his entitlement."

"I swear to you, Nereus, if I ever get out of here, I will fight to see you die a horrid death!" an angry female voice shouted from behind an arched and intricately crafted metal door as they passed.

Rampart's jaw tightened. His gray eyes flashed like the sun bouncing light off the blade of a sword. "How do we get in there?" he growled.

"Like we entered the bars of Ozil's prison," the jinn said, and stepped right through the closed door. With wide eyes, Ozil followed, Rampart close behind.

The room was not large. It had no windows. The walls were bare, the floor cold beneath them. The only furniture was a red velvet chaise lounge and a gold, glided, table. The table held a decanter of wine, a goblet, a platter with cheese and bread, and a small bowl of honey.

Nereus was stretched out on the chaise lounge; honey dripped from a slice of the bread as the Erlking popped it into his mouth. He was not wearing his mask. The imprint of the angel's curse throbbed with the fire beneath it. Nereus's smile stiffened with each ray of pulsing light.

The Erlking sat up and plucked a linen napkin from the table and wiped his mouth. "You will die long before me if you do not accept the invitation to my bed."

"Never!" The faery sat on a tree limb inside a gold, circular cage with vertical and horizontal bars hanging from a chain attached to the ceiling. It sparkled with magic and was within Nereus's reach. "You will have to kill me first." The fae was breathtakingly beautiful. "Over the many years you held me captive, I have never exposed my true anger. My magical powers are strong. They are even stronger when my life is threatened. Up until now, I have never felt this threatened. But still, I do not fear you, Nereus. Do you know why?"

The Erlking reached up and gave the cage a push then laid back and watched it swing back and forth over his head. "Do tell. Your chatter is always an entertainment I cannot do without."

The fae's violet eyes glinted anger over a dainty nose and plump purple lips. She had no body hair and in its stead, intricate lavender tattoos etched markings that glittered on her body everywhere hair or lashes should have been. She wore gold cuffs around ears that came to a point at the upper curve of her head. A scanty shift was cinched with a leather rope around a wisp of a waist. On delicate arms and legs, small tributaries of deep purple veins were barely visible giving off a surreal impression as they pumped life fluids through her body. Lacey wings were tucked tightly behind her body.

"Because I can kill you in a second."

"Why don't you?" Nereus asked. "Or should I say why you haven't then?"

Reka said nothing. Having spent years locked in a wasp nest at his mercy, she found herself once again struggling with an urge to kill him, and she could. But he was not hers to destroy.

Nereus took a sip of wine, stood, and walked to a small fire built in an iron brazier. He picked up a long poker leaning against the wall and stirred the flame until the end of the poker glowed.

"Be careful and be swift this time, Nereus, because when you finally madden me with that poker," the faery solemnly whispered, "I may just impale myself and win this battle by my hand." She gently ran fingers over pocked burn marks on her right shoulder and arm.

The Erlking walked over and laid the glowing end of the poker on one of the bars of the cage. "Do you really want to die, Queen Reka?"

CHAPTER SIX

The Madness of the Erlking

Rampart gritted his teeth as Nereus slowly spun Reka's cage, his hungry eyes examining her at every angle. The wasp queen had long been thought dead by the rebels. Rampart didn't know her very well personally, but her name was affixed with the other legends of the Rebellion. To think, this whole time such a hero to their cause was being held captive by a man who would treat her as a toy in a child's hand. The veil between realities could barely keep Rampart's rage from lashing out at the Erlking.

"Let me out of the Gray," Rampart barked. "I can't allow this kind of depravity to continue."

Aldul remained still.

"I said let me out, damn you!" Rampart allowed his rage to boil over at the jinn.

"You talked me into coming here with the expectations of releasing your captain, and we have done that," Aldul said. "I never agreed to proceed through the castle, freeing everyone being held captive unjustly. I'm already stretching what the jinn had authorized me to do here."

Rampart moved closer to Aldul, ready to argue. The calm hand of Ozil grasped his shoulder. "I appreciate what you've done, Aldul," the captain said. "And I wouldn't ask you to commit to a prison riot, or assassination attempt. But if you could merely distract Nereus for a while, Rampart and I can do the rest."

Aldul watched as the Erlking tapped menacingly on the cage bars. "Well, I suppose I did come here to deliver a message to the king. Hadn't planned on doing it in this setting, but why the hell not? It may prove amusing." The jinn moved behind Nereus. "I will leave the veil open for you when we leave, but without my presence here to maintain the opening, it will close within a few minutes. Work fast; if you aren't able to return to the Gray before Nereus returns, I'm not sure I will be able to save you."

Both fae nodded.

Aldul moved behind Nereus's chaise lounge as the king licked honey from his fingers. The jinn materialized in his smoky form and cleared his throat, causing the Erlking to jump up in alarm.

"Sorry," Aldul said. "Didn't mean to interrupt... whatever this is. There are few ways to emerge from the Gray without startle—"

"—GET OUT!" Nereus snapped. "How dare you enter the Erlking's presence unannounced and uncalled?!"

"Ah yes, I do apologize for arriving without warning. However, I thought with the strained relationship between the fae and jinn, it would be a wiser course of action not to draw attention to my presence in your court. Wouldn't want rumors spreading throughout your land, especially with the turmoil it currently finds itself in."

Nereus scurried to the side table where his mask lay. He scrambled with the leather straps as if caught naked. "You shouldn't be in this land at all, jinn. Nevertheless in my castle, or my private chambers."

"Private chambers?" Aldul said, eyeing Reka in her cage, who returned his gaze with a suspicious look. "Yes, I would say this doesn't appear to be a room I'd find myself invited to."

"Watch your tongue." Nereus fastened the last strap of his mask and turned to face Aldul. "You may feel safe inside your precious Gray, but rest assured I've fought many jinn during the war, and I have my ways of hurting you."

Aldul smiled. "I mean no disrespect, and I'm certainly not here looking to fight you. But I would like to remind you of the fragile peace between our two people, and that attacking a delegate of the jinn could lead to further hostility between our races. Seeing as you're struggling with your own people at the moment, I would think you would wish to avoid that possibility at any cost."

Nereus's nostrils flared, and his eyes narrowed. The mark beneath his mask flared from the thoughts he envisioned. He winced, but his rage burned brighter than the mark.

Aldul clasped his hands behind him, unconcerned with the Erlking's anger. "I was sent to deliver a message from the jinn leadership. If you would allow me to do so, then my business with you will be concluded and you will be free of me."

Nereus clenched his teeth and moved within a few inches of the jinn's smokey face. "Outside," he growled, and walked through the intangible being. Nereus stomped to the door and flung it open. Aldul followed him, but before the door fully closed behind him, he made a subtle gesture to open the veil for the two fae to mount their rescue. Just before the door latched, the jinn saw Rampart and Ozil leap from the Gray. So far, everything was going as they had hoped.

The two walked in silence through the hall and winding staircases. They passed several castle guards on their way. The jinn gathered looks of surprise and anger from them, but Nereus had no reason to be concerned with them knowing of Aldul's presence. No guard under his command would ever consider leaking information of what they saw within the castle walls. Enough examples had been made to ensure that.

Nereus led them to the great hall. Large stone pillars lined the walkway, and a long blue carpet led to the throne where guards waited like statues. Ornate stained-glass windows decorated the walls, their colors dulled under the starless night.

Nereus climbed the stairs to his throne, a large sharply angled chair with the appearance of ice. He sat cross legged with his robes draped across the armrests. "This is where I talk to delegates from foreign lands, jinn." He snarled. "In the name of peace, I will forgive the disrespect you showed earlier. But hear me when I say, approach me again in the same manner and no threat will keep me from ripping the blood from your body."

The Erlking sat with confidence, and the aggravation he showed down in the dungeon faded away. This was where he had threatened countless people who had always bowed to him in the end. Here he had homefield advantage, and no one could touch him.

"Of course." Aldul dropped his head. "Next time I will make sure word is sent of my arrival."

"See that you do," Nereus sneered. "Now, say what you came to say and be gone."

"Certainly, my lord. I have come with good news for your kingdom."

Nereus leaned forward.

"Due to recent events, the jinn have decided to no longer hold the treaty requirements outlined by the now disgraced Talock. Meaning, Your Highness, we will no longer expect you to ban your people from breeding with other races."

The guards shifted in their stance, and the soft clank from their armor cut through the silence like a knife. Nereus's color drained momentarily from his face, then he grew darker than ever before. The light seeping from under his mask pulsed, causing him to wince from pain.

"Give us the room!" he barked at his guards, his eyes locked on Aldul. The sentries quickly clambered out into the hall as if their lives depended on it. And with the Erlking's current mood, they might have. "What are you talking about, jinn? Is this a joke of some kind?"

"No, no joke. We have reevaluated the treaty and found it overly harsh. Thus, no longer felt it necessary to hold you to it." Aldul did his best to produce a polite smile. "And you don't have to keep referring to me as 'jinn'; my name is Aldul."

Nereus lunged to his feet. "I don't give a hot orc shit what your name is! What makes you think the jinn have any right to tell me, the king of this land, what laws I enforce upon my people?!"

Aldul stretched his arms to his sides. "None. What you decide to put into law is your own decision. However, we can state whether or not we will require it in the name of keeping the treaty, which we no longer will." He clasped his smoky hands in front of his stomach. "We thought it would please your highness. The jinn are aware of your dwindling numbers; we thought you would jump at the chance to—"

"I just fought a war with my own people for this treaty," Nereus spat. "And now at the end of it, you come to my castle, unannounced and uninvited, to tell me it is for nothing, then expect me to be pleased?"

Aldul looked around to make sure the hall was emptied. "Are you really going to stand there, king of the fae, and tell me your sole reason for fighting these rebels was due to your respect for our treaty? I might not have been at the signing, but word among my colleagues is you signed the document quicker than a dog would snatch scraps dropped on the floor. Almost would make one think you were happy to subjugate your people and use the evil jinn as an excuse to hold your boot on their necks."

Nereus narrowed his eyes. Even though Aldul couldn't fully materialize in the fae dimension, he could still sense the moisture in the air thickening as the Erlking's power flexed. "I see you feel comfortable speaking freely before me, jinn. You have quite a pair, I'll give you that."

Aldul shrugged. "I just grow tired of the pseudo politeness required of diplomats. It's a silly game we play in order to seem respectful, but since it's just you and me here, I feel it would be a waste of time to dance around the subject, don't you?"

For a moment, Nereus responded with silence. But in a move that surprised Aldul, the Erlking smiled. "Very well, candid speaking it is," he said in a dark tone, stepping closer to hover over the jinn. "Let me guess, the opinion of the jinn have lessened of late, hasn't it? It was no secret many of the races didn't approve of the regulations you implemented over the fae after the war. The rebels here villainized me over the events with the half fae, but that's not how the other species viewed the events, was it?" Nereus smirked and looked down his nose. "No; they saw a king being forced to turn on his own people in order to stay in the guidelines of the treaty your kind forced us to sign. And I'm sure it didn't matter to them just how many jinn agreed with the documents or not. You're all as guilty as Talock was in their eyes. Now you come here expecting me to believe the jinn leadership has sent you here with this message of 'good tiding' out of compassion for the fae people? Ha! I see it for what it is, nothing more than an attempt to swing the public opinion, and others will see through it as well."

"I don't deny there's been pressure on us to change the requirements we've put on the fae people," Aldul said. "The angels have never approved of it and have breathed down our necks ever since the signing. And after your attempted genocide of the half fae, that pressure has only intensified. It's left us with no option than to step back from the situation. Bottom line is, if you wish to keep imposing the ban on procreation with other races, then the fault will be on your shoulders, and yours alone. The jinn will no longer be your patsy."

Nereus growled through bared teeth. He spun on his heel and plopped back onto his throne. "I think not. The ban will continue, and the jinn won't say a word. For if you do, I'll be forced to go to the other races and convince them this conversation never took place. Have you ever tried to match a fae in a war of words? I'll convince them you came here to threaten me into remaining silent on the issue. After all these years of your regulations on my people, do you think any of them will believe you over me, especially considering your people's history? I'll have them eating out of the palm of my hand till I find a new ally. You made your bed, jinn, now you have to lay in it."

The green and gold smoke Aldul was composed of burned brighter. "If you continue the ban under our name, the jinn leadership will become involved in this conflict."

"Then a new war between our people will commence!"

"An empty threat. You can't declare war on my people for the same reason you didn't attack me down in your little dungeon of cruel and inhumane iniquities. If you did you'd find yourself in a battle you couldn't win. This war-torn land is too weak for another war."

The Erlking's laugh echoed down the great hall. "Listen here, demon, I will not bargain, I will not surrender, I WILL NOT bow to the likes of you." A devilish smirk spread across his face. "There was a time I genuinely loved this land and its people, that's why I've worked so hard to try to keep its purity whole. But what have I gotten for bringing peace to this land? Villainized. My name dragged through the mud by a group of weak-minded peasants that can't comprehend the complexity of what I was trying to do. So, I'm done trying to play nice. My enemies will bow at my feet, and I will accomplish that in whatever way necessary. Go ahead, attack us. Storm our realm. I'll see that every village burns, that every fae lay dead in front of your forces before I surrender. And when the smoke clears, the other races will ban together and put an end to you. Because if I can't beat you by force, I'll damn sure drag you to oblivion with me."

The full madness of the Erlking displayed before Aldul was worse than he could have imagined. If the king was truly ready to sacrifice his people in order to maintain power, and Aldul believed him when he said he would, then there would be no negotiation. For when reason was absent, so was hope.

The doors at the end of the hall flew open with a loud thud. A guard ran in so fast he stumbled over the blue carpet. "My lord, I have urgent..."

Nereus gestured and picked the guard up by his wings. With a sharp yank of the hand the guard flew through the air past the pillars and landed hard where Aldul floated. He skidded to a stop when his helmet connected with the bottom stairwell.

"I had asked for the room!" Nereus bellowed. "You dare interrupt your king without being summoned?"

"My apologies, my lord. Please, I beg mercy," the guard said as he scrambled to his knees. "But I bring word from the prison. Ozil and the bee queen, Reka, have escaped their cells. I was told to tell you immediately."

Nereus's fiery eyes turned to Aldul with suspicion. No accusation needed to be made, because as they locked eyes, the Erlking knew somehow the jinn was involved. And since words were no longer needed between the two, Aldul simply smiled and disappeared back fully within the Gray, leaving the king screaming at his guards.

CHAPTER SEVEN

Escape Within a Breath of Gray

"Damn, that was close," Rampart said through a wide smile he did not often wear.

"Gentlemen," Reka said, "you poked Nereus to the outer edge of sanity tonight with Ozil's rescue. My confinement and torture in the golden cage was the Erlking's only soothing concession since the disappearance of half breeds. His daily threats that I would soon bear witness to Ozil's brutalization and slow death are what kept Ozil alive. I have no doubt many would have witnessed my torment tomorrow, and days after, until my headless body was skewered on a pole outside the castle. I am forever in your debt for rescuing both of us, Aldul, but I fear the Erlking's rage will excel to a frenzied killing spree of innocent fae. I can't be the object of his rage."

"I will not leave you here alone," Rampart said. "If you stay, I will join you."

Reka and Rampart stood facing each other in halls darkened by the Gray. The Erlking's rage echoed off the walls around them.

Ozil did not miss the fear for her people in Reka's violet eyes as she struggled with a decision she was desperately trying to make. A soft blue glow of color rose in patches on her otherwise white cheeks. Translucent wings lied limp over her back and shoulders like another layer of skin. And still, her beauty was magnetic.

"We will stop him, Reka," Ozil said. "Nereus has inappropriately crossed the lines of rationality too often as of late. Many of the fae that once supported him can no longer ignore the deaths of innocent friends and neighbors at his command. And if Nereus does as you say, the fae are sure to scatter to protect themselves."

"Ozil is correct, Reka," Rampart said. "The fae will rally with us. Especially with Ozil and you at our sides, and the news of the jinn breaking the treaty Nereus made with Talock will soon be public. Help us end this."

Aldul had been quiet and stood patiently while the others spoke but now his lips were tight, and his eyes scanned the stairs and hallway. "We must move, fae Reka. Choose wisely. I will open the Gray for you to exit but will go no further. Know that it was not my choice to rescue you. I only fulfilled Rampart's requests for Ozil and then you. I do not regret doing so. But we must get back to camp."

Reka ruffled her white skinned, bat-like wings and bowed her head. The Erlking's rants were closer now. It was clear Nereus was headed toward them and the room Reka had been captive in. When she turned and headed down a stairway leading them away from the Erlking, they followed. They raced down damp, drafty halls, and cobblestoned stairs toward a starless sky. Housemaids and cleaning staff with fear in their eyes, and shocked expressions on their faces, peeked from cracked chamber doors and swiftly closed them again.

"I say damn him to an early death," Reka hissed. "Finally, I will be beside you in battle again, Ozil."

Ozil beamed with happiness, his wings helping him keep up. "To finally get you back from a beehive I had so diligently guarded for years, to once again stand beside me in battle gives hope to a new future for all of us."

Rampart gave Ozil a side glance. "You never told me Reka was a fighter."

"And a damn good one," Ozil said, eyes sparkling as he turned a corner and flew down the last passageway alongside the others. "She was my first guard."

"I was her replacement?" Rampart asked.

"Yes. Reka has a frightening, yet powerful magic. This you will see." Ozil's eyes moved to Reka. "I have missed you, friend."

Reka's lavender tattoos pulsed on her hairless head, shoulders, and arms. "And I you."

"If you are as powerful as Ozil says," Aldul said, "why didn't you fight Nereus, Reka?"

"Nereus has always been cruel and frightening, yet he managed to hang on to an edge of his sanity because of me. Nereus wanted me to succumb to his sexual degeneracies like all the other fae he had bullied to do so. When I refused, it became a game with him. One he did not wish to lose. That was my destiny.

"Fighting him with magic powers instead of his own weakness would have been foolish. It would not have ended well. I knew if I agreed to his sexual debauchery there would be others after me. Winning my consent was the battle, not the end result. There were many before me, but none refused him more than once. Nereus could have spoiled all of us by using force but doing so would not have been *his* win. That's why he concentrated only on me with his insults and attempted humiliations. His forced imprisonment in a hive I could have escaped years ago became a larger thorn in my side when Nereus used Ozil, my Captain, to guard and keep me there. But I held strong. Even when the Erlking caged me in the castle after Ozil was imprisoned for refusing to obey his commands to kill all the half breeds, I stayed strong. And tonight, I am free because it was your choice. And at this point, I am not what Nereus needs to quell his insanity."

"So, you see, Aldul," Ozil said, "tonight's events will drive the Erlking's madness into a fury only death will untemper. He has lost three battles, my execution, the jinn's refusal to honor the treaty, and Reka's final rejection."

Reka stood still, eyes on the only way out for her now. "It is time. A different lunacy has taken over the Erlking since the Watcher's curse branded his face. He drifts in and out of madness. He cannot be trusted. It's time to fight him on even ground where I can use my powers."

Together, they walked through a wall on the north side of the castle and Aldul said, "For your safety, I'll accompany you in the Gray to your camp. As for me, I have done enough damage tonight. I will go to my people with this new information and the happenings of my trip. Hopefully they will agree that they, once again, need to assist with the fate of the fae world."

"I wonder if we should contact the angels," Rampart said.

Outside of the castle, wind howled and blew tree branches, sailing leaves in the open air beyond the curtains of the Gray. The jinn stood with the others in solid form. Wind howled and blew their hair and wings. The dew-covered grass was not damp under their feet. Guards stood against the castle walls ten feet apart for as far as they could see, but the group went unnoticed.

Every muscle in Aldul's body was taught. "It is sad to consider your people need jinn and angels to solve this, but after witnessing recent events I believe it is true. Tonight, sleep. You all need a good rest before planning your next move.

"I'll sleep good tonight," Ozil said. "I'm free because of you and Rampart."

"I will not forget this," Rampart said as they moved through the night. "I still owe *you* two wishes, Aldul. Tell your people that."

"No. My actions are mine. But on a personal level, I will remember this," Aldul said, a smile returning to his face.

***

Coralina sat by a crackling fire, after a long day. She had magicked the rest of the caravan with a sleep spell. Nothing will wake them but the fog of the morning. The supplies she and Dusk pilfered from Copper Groves were inventoried and packed away where no otherworld horrors could get to them. Her day would have been done as well if it were not for the absence of Rampart.

“It’s getting late, hound,” Coralina said. “Where the hell are they? I have a burning desire to head to the castle.”

“And should you let it take you in that direction, it would surely turn into a hell of a mistake.” Dusk was on his side, back close to the fire. “Nereus gives fae a bad name. You know it’s fear that his breed is becoming more powerful than him, right?”

“Always has been,” Coralina said. “That and he’s a sadistic masochist. With a narcistic hatred for women.”

“And you’re a big-ass threat.” Dusk yawned, eyes closed, tongue creeping over his lower teeth. “He dies, you take over the throne. Everything he hates.”

“I’m not a half breed.” Coralina poked the fire with a stick.

“No, just his mortal enemy,” Dusk said laced with sarcasm. “Aren’t you glad I’m here to protect your loyal butt?”

“You know *your* butt is a hare’s breath away from catching fire, right?” Coralina said. “I could use my fae born gift to stoke the fire instead of this stick.” Ash twirled the fiery end around in front of his nose.

Dusk snorted. “Please do. My fur doesn’t burn; smolder maybe, but I like the heat at night. Aren’t you chilled?”

“Only with the thought that Rampart and the others may be in danger.”

A loud hiss and falling branches had them on their feet. Tree limbs cracked and fell to the ground around them. A large snake poked it’s head up over the treetops like a black periscope with a white belly. It tilted its head, hissed, and glared through glowing yellow eyes. A forked tongue caught the firelight and flashed florescent green as the huge creature hissed again and dropped its flattened, arrow shaped head closer.

“Holy shit!” Coralina said, and put the fire between her and the snake. “Do you see that?”

"Yeah," Dusk said, still cozying up to the flames. "Nothing like a Grootslang to screw up a perfectly lovely evening on Hell's doorstep."

"Time to drag out your embodied guardian and servant of hell," Coralina said, "or whatever demon is ruling your roost."

"Oh, stop. Get your wings flapping and help me kill our main food source for the next month or two."

"Are you fucking kidding me?" Coralina shook her head, mouth open. "I'm not eating that!"

The snake dropped its head closer and opened its mouth large enough to swallow Dusk in one bite.

Dusk stood and barked as though teasing it to strike. When it dropped its head closer and hissed louder, the hellhound leapt and dug his incisors into the snake's neck. The Grootslang shook a head the size of one of their caravan wagon's wheels, twirled its tail around Dusk, and squeezed. The Grootslang opened its mouth wider, reared back its head, and hissed again.

"A little help here!" Dusk choked out.

Coralina flattened her palm, aimed it at the fire, and sent a whirlwind that gathered dirt, rocks, and charred and flaming wood into a mini tornado. Then with a flip of her hand the tornado was airborne. Seconds later, it was inside the mouth of the Grootslang. The snake went crazy, head flipping, body knocking down large tree limbs, and lost its grip on Dusk.

Coralina held her hand firm to force the ball of fire further down the throat of the snake. The Grootslang looked like a slow falling tree with bulging elongated pupils and a swollen neck. Dusk hit the dirt, and rolled away from the reptile's head as it hit the ground in a black cloud of dirt. When the dirt settled, the Grootslang lay motionless at their feet.

"I'm definitely not field dressing that thing, never mind eat it," Coralina said, and rubbed soot off her face and arms.

"Do I look like I have hands?" Dusk asked, body shaking from maw to tail in amusement. "And someone should pick up all the wood and stack it in one of the wagons."

"Not tonight," Coralina said, her spit sooty as she spat. "And please don't shake again. My mouth is gritty."

"Yeah, mine too. Deal with it," Dusk said. "Seems we have to wait till morning since you knocked out the rest of the fae for the night." Dusk snorted at what was left of the fire. "Talk about stupidity."

"Alright. I'll give you that," Coralina said. "It probably wasn't a good move to knock everyone out."

"Ya think?" Dusk said. "Toss a few logs on the fire, will ya? No matter what Rampart said, I am not sitting in the cold with you and a dead snake while you wait for him to get back."

"Rampart asked you to do that?" Coralina hesitantly toed the snake.

"No." Dusk rolled his fiery red eyes back until they showed a sliver of white. "I just said that for the hell of it." He shook again from head to tail and slung drool that sizzled as it hit what was left of their campfire. "I can't believe you haven't eaten Grootslang."

"Don't change the subject." Coralina tossed a few pieces of wood on the remaining fire and then blew just enough wind to crank it up. She glared at Dusk as she flopped down near the fire.

"I'm not. All this drama is your attraction, camouflaged with annoyance. Not mine," Dusk said. He flopped down by the fire and studied the snake. "We're lucky tonight. Grootslang is good eating."

"I'm sure it would be if I were a slimeball, scavenging hellhound."

"Suit yourself," Reka said as she landed in the ring of light created by the fire. "More for us."

Coralina jumped to her feet.

Reka put up her hand. "Calm down. Aldul and Rampart rescued me *and* Ozil. The men stopped to bid the jinn farewell. I couldn't wait to see you again."

Coralina grinned. "Oh, hell yes! I am so glad to see you, Queen Reka. I hope you brought a fighting spirit with you."

"It is time. And you can stop calling me a queen," Reka said, "because I'm ready to fight, just like you."

"And what are your powers?" Dusk asked.

Coralina froze. She never heard what Reka was capable of. No one knew, and no one ever asked. Until now.

Reka's breasts rose and fell with a deep breath she took in through her nose and then exhaled with a sigh. "I was going to wait until I could tell everyone in the morning. I guess I owe you an answer, my friend.

"I am an anomaly," Reka said. "My father was the only surviving child of Caorthannach, the Celtic fire spitter. As the legend goes, Angels chased my grandmother from her lair beneath Lough Derg with the help of the heavens, and my father was among many of her living children hidden in the lair. They then sent a great wind into the caves to eradicate all of them. My father was the only survivor and escaped to Faery Lands on the shoulder of the demon that saved him. That's where he met my mother, a water fae, and they mated. Both of them were killed in the great war. I was used as a changeling on earth because of my father's hatred for the Erlking. But Nereus found out and dragged me back. He has always misjudged my powers and the rest is history you well know."

"Wow," Coralina said. "And I thought my lineage was a horror story."

Reka laughed.

"You still haven't told us what your powers are," Dusk said.

"I'm a fire spitter with the ability to control liquids." Reka's eyes moved from the hellhound to Coralina. "Go ahead. I know you are going to ask."

When Coralina said nothing, Dusk did. "Yeah, so I'm thinking fire and water don't work together well unless you're brewing a good soup."

"One would think," Reka said with a smile. "But my inherited gifts were enhanced by the love my parents shared for each other. It goes without saying I'm capable of putting out fires." She paused, and when Dusk snorted with amusement, she added, "I can turn lakes, streams, rivers, rain...and...*any* bodily fluid into fire. I could melt your brain, Hellhound."

***

"What will you tell your people?" Rampart asked the jinn as they stood in the Gray by the fence that separated the Bad Lands from Faery Lands.

"I will tell them the Erlking is demented with the fire curse of an appointed Watcher, and Nereus's removal from the throne might be our only way to prevent another war between the three most powerful realms in the Otherworld."

"And if that doesn't work?" Ozil asked.

"Then it may be time to ask the heavens to join us."

CHAPTER EIGHT

Fae Hope and Despair

The caravan moved through the densest parts of the forest to avoid the attention of the guard. It had been two weeks since Ozil and Reka were rescued. For the first few days the rebels had held their breath, waiting for guardsmen to start barreling through the forest in full force. But none came. As the day passed without sighting any spies in the area, many around camp began to relax, figuring the Erlking didn't see the freeing of two prisons as need for retaliation. However, Coralina knew any offense against Nereus would entice his need for retribution. He would make an example of anyone who challenged him. So while the tension in camp lessened, Coralina's increased, knowing the longer it took for his ire to crash upon them, the more heinous it would be.

Fortunately, the company's morale had been at its highest ever since the fall of Copper Grove. For the first time since arriving in the Bad Lands, everyone was well fed, even though the Grootslang was tough and tasteless. Many of the soldiers celebrated the return of Captain Ozil. And the arrival of Reka brought a new hope, for if someone caught in the Erlking's clutches as long as she could break free, they could, too. Rampart wanted to capitalize on that emotion and sent Ozil, Reka, and several other messengers to nearby villages looking for recruits. It was a risky endeavor. If they ran into a town loyal to the Erlking, not only could the messenger be harmed, but the caravan would be at risk of discovery as well. So Coralina ordered the camp to stay mobile, and under the shelter of the forest canopy to keep from the eye of crow riding guardsmen.

Rampart's efforts had shown good results. There were several small settlements deep in the Bad Lands that had ignored the Erlking's order for civilians to move closer to the city. The guard rarely traveled far and wide enough into the Bad Lands, so they felt safer in their defiance to stay at their homeland. Luckily for the rebels, that also meant there was less chance of finding loyalists among them. Several new pledges had joined them since recruitment began. They were still far away from the numbers needed to storm the castle, but it showed interest in the rebellion wasn't dead.

Coralina hovered in front of the convoy scouting the path. Two other faeries with earth powers flanked her, smoothing the ground and peeling away the brushes so the wagons could get through. Two other earth magic fae followed behind to return the path to its original form and cover their tracks. The brush was thick, and traveling was slow. But if it was hard for them, it would be hard for their pursuers as well.

Coralina saw a bead of sweat tumble off the chin of the fae to her left. "Do you need a break?"

The earth fae shook her head. "There's only a few hours of daylight left," she said through labored breaths. "We don't have time to waste with breaks. I'll be fine."

"We don't have time to waste picking your ass off the forest floor when you pass out either," Coralina said, "but I'll trust you to let me know before that happens."

Coralina couldn't help but smile. It was good to see the determination return to her people. After weeks of hanging heads around camp, the rebel fae walked with purpose again.

In the distance, Coralina saw movement beneath the treetops. Her senses immediately went on alert until she saw the iridescent body of a dragonfly approaching. It was Rampart's way of communicating with her. Usually, he'd attach a letter explaining how diplomacy with the villages went, and how many volunteers he'd recruited. Coralina furrowed her brow. Rampart had just left to meet with the leaders of Ensley, a small village just a few hours from where they were. With Dusk's speed they would have had time to get there, but there was no way he'd have any news to report yet. It stood hairs up on the back of her neck. Early news was never good news.

The insect, her equal in size, flew up and hovered in front of Coralina. The fast beating of its wings was strong enough to blow her back a couple of inches. She reached out delicately and plucked the paper letter attached between its thorax and abdomen. When she unfolded it, there was only a short message within.

Coralina, come quickly to Ensley, and send word to Reka and Ozil.

Rampart wasn't a man of few words; if he rushed to send the letter, Coralina knew that wasn't a good sign. She checked to make sure Rampart's seal was on the bottom before attaching it again to the dragonfly. "Take the message to Ozil and Reka," she said before turning to the sweating earth fae. "I have to go to meet Rampart. You two tell the convoy to stop and hunker down here for the night. I won't be able to get back till dawn." Before they could respond, Coralina took off toward Ensley.

She was tired from the long day of work, but traveling at top speed, the village was only two hours away. The horrible thoughts dancing in her head pushed her forward. If Rampart had been ambushed by the guard, he didn't have any support to fight them off. It was too hard for large groups to travel without gaining suspicion, so most recruiters travel alone or with a partner. Rampart only had Dusk with him. While they were a deadly team, even a hellhound had its limits. Other scenarios swarmed her thoughts, each one worse than the next, until she soon found herself within sight of Ensley.

At first, nothing seemed out of the ordinary. However, when she drew near she saw scorch marks on buildings. Walls laid in rubble as if they were torn down and smeared across the streets. Some roofs were peeled off like can lids. Bent backward or thrown to the sides. Coralina's heart skipped a beat. She dropped to the forest floor and slowly approached on foot while she kept an eye out for hidden enemies in the brush. As Coralina drew closer to the village, she saw the silhouette of Rampart on the path, his wings hung low on his back. Without thinking, she rushed toward him. The worry she felt faded away. Even though something happened here, he was fine, and that meant more to her than she wanted to admit.

"Rampart," she called to him. "Are you okay?"

He turned with an expression on his face she hadn't seen before. His smile at seeing her hid sadness. His eyes focused on hers, yet they were hazy, as if unfocused. "I'm fine," Rampart said. "I got here after it happened."

Coralina drew in closer and ran her fingertips down the back of his bare arm and under his elbow. "Do you know what happened?" she asked softly.

"Yeah, that's what we'd like to know." The male voice came from behind her.

Coralina quickly removed her hand from Rampart's arm and felt the heat of her flushing cheeks as she turned to see Ozil and Reka rushing toward them.

"I'm not sure; the town was already ravaged before I got here." Rampart hung his head. "When I saw the results, I sent for Coralina immediately. Walk with me."

Rampart headed down the path and into the village with the others following close behind. They walked past empty, dark houses. The silence was unnerving. Coralina had visited this area a few months ago. The people here were joyous, and there was always music blaring from the town square. Now there was nothing but burnt wood and the smell of ash.

As they approached the square, Coralina became aware of figures lying on the ground. Lantern light flickered off rows of bodies lying face down in the dirt. Dozens of them. Men, woman, and children all placed neatly in columns around the square. Each one had their left wing cut off at the base, and their arms spread out to touch the fingertips of the body next to them.

The four of them stood there for a moment, taking the gruesome scene in. Every citizen of the village laid before them, disfigured and left in the open. "Why would they do this?" Reka asked in a hollow voice. "Just because they refused to move to the castle?"

"No," a male voice came from behind. "Because of me."

The party turned swiftly to see Calastair step out of the building's shadows. His silver eyes fixed on the body of a brown-haired child. He walked aimlessly toward the group, as if he was unaware of anyone's presence before him. His red hair glowed like an unburning fire.

"Cal?" Reka asked. "What are you doing here?"

"I've been keeping up on what's been happening since the revolution began," he said, his gaze remained fixed ahead. "All of the angels have been watching closely, especially when atrocities like this occur."

Coralina clenched her jaw but said nothing.

"It's good to see you, my friend," Ozil said. "But, hold on. Why is this because of you?"

Cal's shoulders slumped. "I think the Erlking is sending messages to his enemies in the only way his hateful heart knows how to." The angel turned to show them his right wing, and the stump of his left one. "I don't take it as a coincidence Nereus cut all their left wings off just like me, the angel who branded him."

Rampart shook his head. "Wait, that doesn't make sense. Why now? After everything that has happened recently, why would he suddenly be targeting you?"

Cal sighed. "I said he's sending a message to his enemies, plural, not just me." His eyes looked at Ozil. "The town of Olette was destroyed. Its people were hung upside down and left to die, and the fae symbol for 'captain' was carved on their foreheads." He shifted to Reka. "The people of Pavia were poisoned with wasp toxin similar to the one your soldiers used to protect you." There was a pause in his voice as he looked at Coralina. "Then there was the town of Tryamon, where the first-born daughters were taken from their families and hung in front of all to see."

Coralina's unflinching eyes matched Cal's gaze till he shied away from them.

"Nereus has lost his mind," Cal continued. "He's blinded by rage and frustration. He'll burn everything and everyone to the ground before giving up his rule. It's not enough for him to just win the war; he wants to crush the rebellion so bad no one would ever think about challenging him again. And these people are just tools for him to use against those who oppose him."

Rampart clenched his teeth. "There's a lot of people on that list."

"And a lot of fae left to torture and kill," Cal said. "He'll probably even try to spin it to those around the castle that the rebellion is responsible for all the deaths. And, unfortunately, some will believe it."

Rampart paced quickly, fingers running against his scalp as he pulled and tugged on his hair. "Well, that's it, we have to gather the forces and storm the Erlking's keep, right now. He wants to make us look like monsters? Then let's give him the monstrous adversaries he makes us out to be. We'll rip him from his cushy bed and drag him through the streets!"

"Calm down," Ozil barked.

"Calm down?! Are you kidding me?" Rampart continued to manically pace. "I'm not going to wait while he decides which town he wants to decimate in my honor. What do you think he'll do, burn it down? Yeah, that makes sense, right? Imps like fire. Or maybe he'll come up with something a little more creative, like hunting down everyone from my home village. To hell with that!"

Ozil stepped within Rampart's pacing track. "I taught you better than this," he said with a strong voice. "Nereus is doing this to get into our heads. Instead, we need to wrap our heads around this. As horrible as it is, we can't act impulsively. We'd be led to the slaughter if we stormed into the capital without a plan."

Rampart took a deep breath. "Look, of course we're not going to do that. I needed to vent, rage, release steam. Damn him, I'm beyond furious! With that being said, we don't have time to wait around anymore. We all know what Nereus is capable of, and this won't be the end of his madness. If we don't respond to these slaughters like he wants, he'll just keep ramping up the terrors he'll unleash."

"He's right," Cal said. "Nereus isn't going to stop till you surrender, or he forces you to play into his hand. At this point, he has the advantage, and he'll work it to push you into making a mistake. We can't wait but can't act impulsively either."

Coralina raised an eyebrow. "We?" she said, icy gaze set upon Cal. "What do you mean by 'we'? I thought you weren't allowed to get involved with our war, some bullshit angel rule about interference."

"Yeah, well... his killing of these people as a way to get back at me changes that," Calastair said hesitantly.

Coralina knowingly nodded. "I see, so the slaughter of the fae people was fine up till this point, huh?"

The group looked stunned by her words. All except Calastair, who looked at her with a stone expression.

"This kind of atrocity has been happening for a while now," she continued. "Everyone who's joined our struggle has lost friends and family, yet the angels don't interfere. Copper Groves burned and the iridescent lake boiled, but the angels don't interfere. And now that he's finally taken aim at you, he's gone too far?"

"Cor!" Rampart blurted, but instantly backed off. He'd never used her nickname in front of the others. Doing so now brought red to his cheeks and a stern expression from Coralina.

"IF you want to help, help us bury these people," she said. "To at least show them some kind of respect in death." With that, she turned on her heel and marched back the way she came.

Reka and Rampart glanced at each other, both sharing a shocked expression at Coralina's outburst. Ozil seemed surprised as well, but in typical Ozil fashion, he shrugged it off. Kneeling next to the body of a young girl, he placed his hand gently on her back. "Well, she's certainly right about one thing, these people don't deserve to be left out in the open for display."

"We can work tonight to gather them outside the village," Reka said. "Then in the morning we'll bring the earth fae here to help bury them."

As the two of them began working to move the bodies, Rampart stayed behind. "I don't get it," he said to Calastair. "I thought you and Coralina were friends?"

Cal sighed. "We are. She's just angry. And she has her reasons to be," he said, chewing on the inside of his cheek. "Look, it's fine. I'll go talk with her, then I'll come back and help you guys out, ok?"

Rampart looked down the ally, then back at Cal before nodding.

***

Calastair walked the darkened path, empty houses looming hauntingly in the night. Coralina stood at the edge of town, looking out at the surrounding hills. She didn't turn as he approached.

"I'm not here to fight with you, Coralina," he said in a calm voice. "We did enough of that last time we talked. I wish I could explain why the angels don't interfere with the injustices of other lands. If I could, I would've been by your side all this time. You know that."

Coralina dropped her gaze.

"I look at all the things that have happened on Earth over the years and wonder how much the angels could have stopped. I don't know why angels allow things like that to happen when they could easily stop it. But I've learned over the years, there's just some things we aren't meant to understand."

Coralina sighed and turned to face him. "I don't buy into that nonsense. You guys could have easily stopped all this from happening if you came down from your ivory tower. With that power, why not use it to stomp out the corrupted like Nereus?"

"There are many leaders across many worlds that rule in a way we don't agree with. Should we remove them all from power?"

"As long as it's for the better good, why not?"

"And then what? Hold all the lands under our thumbs? At what point do the saviors become the tyrants? We can't just impose our will on everyone. Then we're no better than the rest of the oppressors."

Coralina gritted her teeth. "We've had this conversation before, Cal. Bottom line is we're not going to agree. And it doesn't matter. In the end, it doesn't change anything. You were here two years ago when this all started. You were the person who spearheaded the evacuation of the half fae and stood by my side when this all began. But as soon as we started the revolution, you left. When I needed you most, you weren't there. And let's not forget, you were the one who torched half of Nereus's face. Which, as amusing as I might find that, has made him even more unstable."

Coralina walked to a building and leaned against it, her chest heavy and shoulders hunched. Suddenly, she looked tired, as if the weight of the last few years all crashed down upon her at once. "Look, I know why you did what you did, and that you hadn't agreed to get involved in a revolution when you came here to help the half fae. I don't blame you, I really don't. It's just, there are times I feel so lost. So many people have died because of what I started. A few years ago, I was in Perdition, trying my hardest to keep to myself. Now I'm in charge of hundreds of people, but still feel just as alone. It's so... crushing."

Calastair leaned against the wall beside her. "You don't carry that responsibility alone. You have Rampart, Ozil, and the fae Reka."

"Yeah, and I'm very grateful for them. But I just can't stop from thinking back to that day at the Conclave, after the half fae were brought there. I talked them into fighting back, when all they wanted was to find a new home. Maya even shook my hand." She kicked at the dirt under her feet. "I suppose you heard she died last year."

Cal leaned the back of his head against the wall. "Yeah."

The pair stood in silence as the cool night air swept through the dead village.

"I keep telling my people that we can still win this war," Coralina said. "Can we, or am I just being a stubborn fool who refuses to surrender, just like my father?"

Cal scoffed. "Well, first of all, you don't have anything in common with Nereus. And second, yes, I fully believe you can win. And I think Nereus does, too. Why else would he be trying so hard to lure you out of hiding? He's desperate to end this now. And that can only mean one thing, that he considers you a threat."

A hint of a smile formed in the corner of Coralina's mouth. "If you're here to help, then we will welcome it. After all, we'll need all the guns we can get when we storm the throne."

***

It was the dead of night when Efrian was awoken by the Erlking bursting into his room. Even in his tired state, the head guardsman sprang to his feet. The king had never entered his chambers before, and his presence now could only mean very good, or more likely, very bad news.

"My lord," Efrian said, dropping to one knee. "How can I be of service?"

"Rise and follow." The Erlking's usual commanding and intense voice was different tonight. It almost sounded gleeful. A severe tone shift from the last few weeks. Ever since the prisoners' escape, Nereus had been in an even fouler mood than normal. To the point where being summoned to his chambers was almost certain death.

Without explanation, The Erlking swiveled and quickly walked out of the room. Efrian barely had time to grab his robe before scurrying after him. The two walked in silence through the castle. Efrian wanted to ask where they were going but didn't dare out of the risk Nereus would take it as him questioning his orders. They walked down into the lowest part of the castle and into the catacombs below. Efrian's bioluminescent skin shinned a neon green light upon the walls, showing lodged bones and skulls glaring at them as they walked past. The pathway led to an underground river that spiraled downward. They followed this river till they entered a giant cavern twice the size of the capital city.

Nereus whispered an incantation into his lantern flame. The light leapt forth from the candle within and shot to the middle of the cavern. Its intensity increased till the outlines of the rock walls were visible. In front of them was a thin overhang, and below the river poured into a lake that completely covered the cavern floor. The light shimmered off the water like silver.

"Do you know what this is?" Nereus asked.

Efrian cleared his throat. "Yes, it's the lake of life," he answered nervously.

Nereus nodded. "Correct. The great subterrain lake that feeds into the water table under our glorious forest. Every plant, every leaf, is given water by this very lake. That's why the first Erlking built the castle here. He claimed, 'this lake is the heart of the forest, the king will be the heart of the people.'"

Nereus stepped out onto the overhang. "This land is in chaos, Captain. The rebels continue infesting minds with their traitorous words. They endanger our people, and the forest with the rebellion. The longer it goes on, the more fae will fall." A toothy smile shined in the low light. "I can't let it go on, and I'm done showing these traitors mercy. And just as this lake gives life to the forest, it will be the instrument to the survival of our people."

The Erlking waved his hand over the edge of the cliff. "You see, every day I will pull more and more water out of the forest and into the lake. The outer edges of the forest will show the effects first. As the plants wither away, the circle will tighten, leaving nowhere for the rebels to hide. I'll draw every drop from the forest if I must, the rebellion will surrender, or watch everything die around them. Then once they are disposed of, I'll return the water, giving life back to the forest."

Efrian's jaw dropped. He didn't dare question his king, but the fae needed the forest to survive. It was their home, their protection, and their food source. Tampering with such a delicate balance was dangerous.

Nereus laughed and glanced at his Captain. "You should consider yourself lucky. Few have been given the privilege of witnessing the true power of their Erlking." He waved his hands over the water and drew them upward. With the simple movement, the cavern shook. The water bubbled beneath them, and the thunder of water crashing against the rock walls was deafening. Slowly, the dark water began to rise, roiling in protest. Rocks fell from the ceiling and caused the lake to splash up the cave walls.

Light from beneath Nereus's mask seeped from its edges, it's intensity almost matching the light from the center of the cavern. The pain was extraordinary, yet Nereus laughed. "Burn me to the bone, scar me beyond recognition," he yelled into the void of the cavern. "I bend a knee to no one. This forest, it's people, are mine to do with as I please, and no angel or demon will ever take that away. I am Nereus, Erlking of the faeries, and you fear me."

CHAPTER NINE

A Turn of the Screw

Efrian was a kind and humble man, an obedient soldier under the Erlking's rule, and one of Ozil's guardsmen.

In the past, Efrian traveled back and forth from his modest dwelling not far from the castle where his wife, two sons, and a daughter lived. Since the rebellion started, he had often been ordered to remain in the castle but made frequent trips to check on his family. For the last six months, Efrian was allowed no trips home, and in the previous three weeks was forbidden to send word and check on their condition. This put a large strain on the head guardsman and haunted his dreams.

It was well into the morning when Efrian rose. He had spent the night with unpleasant scenarios of his family's demise flashing through his mind until he finally opened his eyes. While awake, he would allow no fear of their wellbeing other than the concern that his wife had not received the monies he sent home monthly.

For his family's sake, he did nothing to inquire, lest the Erlking discover and assume disrespect and a lack of loyalty on his part. That would surely incite Nereus's madness. Efrian was forced to live with, and concern himself with, only the Erlking's beckoning call. A lack of respect grew in his heart with each day, and so Efrian developed an intense inability to remain devoted.

By noon, the head guardsman paced his small room adjacent to the Erlking's chambers. Efrian forced his eyes to remain on block floors, cold, damp, and gray as he took eight strides to get from one barren block wall to the other while passing his cot, wardrobe, and small bedside stand that held a washbowl, pitcher, and his toiletries atop.

He could smell the chamber pot that lay on the floor beside the cot. The only outside view was a magicked arrow slit eight feet above the bedside stand. And while lying under the one blanket offered him, and his head at the foot of the cot, all that was visible was the darkened fae sky.

The magic restricted Efrian from flying out into the night, a torturous action by the Erlking in all unguarded wall openings with the exception of Nereus's private and secretive chambers. But those entries were heavily guarded at all times.

A knock at the large wooden door to his bedsit startled him. Disparaging thoughts of his family dissolved and were replaced with anger. The Erlking was out in the village around the castle with twenty-four guards, Efrian's guards, while he himself was asked to stay and keep an eye open in their leave. Something was not right.

Efrian's cleated boots echoed as he stomped toward the door, half expecting the executioner's guards on the other side. He yanked the heavy wooden door open to find a delicate little fae with wide open eyes and a comely body. Her name was Ova and she had been one of Queen Mabyn's favored chamber maids. Now the fae worked in the kitchen. The Queen of the castle hadn't been seen since the day the Erlking captured Reka and moved her from her hive in the forest to the castle. This, in itself, created more tension among the staff. Efrian became part of the disdain when Ozil was arrested and he was appointed Head Guard.

Ova stepped over the threshold with a tray. She passed Efrian, head bowed, but he could see the fear in her eyes. She placed the breakfast tray on the foot of his bed, bent and picked up the chamber pot, and turned to leave.

Efrian closed the door and stood in front of it, blocking Ova's exit. Boldly, he asked, "Have you news of Queen Mabyn's disappearance?"

"No, sir," she said, eyes studying the tips of Efrian's boots over the foul smell of his excrements.

"You do not need to fear me, Ova. I am only concerned for our queen. No one has seen her and I wondered…"

Ova lifted her head and locked eyes with the head guardsman. She studied his expression as her chest rose and fell with a swiftness that indicated uncertainty.

"I know you don't trust me," Efrian slowly said. "It's fear you wear behind your eyes. I am growing more distraught with the Erlking's sanity, lately. I was hoping if the queen was still alive, she would assist me in helping to save her people."

Ova blinked, dropped her shoulders, and moved her eyes to the chamber pot. "She is alive, sir. I bring her food every midday."

"My desire is to free her. Where is she?"

"Imprisoned in a cell below the castle where few tread," Ova said. 'It's guarded now but was never used in the past."

"Would you like me to place that outside the door?" Efrian reached for the chamber pot and Ova handed it to him.

"Thank you, sir."

Efrian cracked the door and glanced up and down the empty hallway. "Does the queen's guard sit outside of the cell?" he asked as he set the pot outside the door.

"No," Ova said as the Erlking's number one guard closed the door and turned to face her. "Saul, he… The guard is stationed above her. "

Efrian saw something in Ova's eyes at the familiarity in using the guard's first name. It wasn't shame. There was definitely a strong connection between she and Saul. He wondered if it was friendship or physical. He nodded for the chambermaid to continue.

"Saul and I are the only two who know of Queen Mabyn's whereabouts. We've been threatened with a slow and painful death if anyone finds out."

Ah, maybe the connection is merely survival. "I believe both of you will be safe. The Erlking will deem fae consorting with the other side responsible, as he did for Ozil's breakout. It gains him political headway." *And a need to murder other innocent townsfolk.* His gut tightened.

Efrian knew the Erlking's actions could no longer be judged, but he also knew that a word or two carefully purported would direct the blame elsewhere if Nereus had something to gain from it.

Ova's chest now rose and fell at a normal pace but fear remained present in her eyes. Efrian knew she was weighing her options against the probability that she had already said too much. He, in turn, had the same reservations.

"I'm worried about my own family," Efrian said. "I have not seen or been allowed to contact them for months."

Ova's forehead wrinkled, her mouth tightened, and her eyes feigned questionable concern as to the nature of a response. He dared not encourage a need for physical comfort and used his words wisely. "I am sure all is well with them today, but my concern is with our unstable Erlking and his inability to control the madness that has come over him. So before it is too late for all of us, including our queen, please trust me, Ova. Your information is as safe with me as I hope mine is with you."

"It is, sir." Ova continued with a respectful camaraderie to her voice. "It's dark where the queen is. It smells horrid with her own excrements, and Saul," she lowered her head again, "well, he said he thought the Erlking...he...relieves himself into her cell."

Ova raised rosy, red cheeks. "There is no arrowslit in the wall or anywhere on the level where she is held, and she is given no candlelight." Each word chased the next as Ova continued. "Queen Mabyn is not allowed a chamber pot, blankets, or even straw or hay for comfort. I was ordered to bring only one meal a day, broth and bread." Ova pulled her eyes from his again. "But I often bring her more. The guard does not stop me. I hide damp rags under my skirts, sir, and extra food in my apron pockets."

Efrian smiled. "You are a good woman, Ova. And loyal to your queen."

"I wish I could do more, sir. I could speak—"

"No!" Efrian said, and immediately regretted the intensity of his word. "Please. Stay silent. And I need you to keep this conversation between us." Efrian raised his hand as Ova opened her mouth to speak. "Saul must not know. It is bad enough that I asked you for your help. I won't bring in another."

"I understand, sir, but—"

"I plan to rescue her immediately. Nereus will not be back until day kicks darkness. We must hurry. I want to be back before the moons show their faces."

Ova grabbed the guard's hands and brought them to her lips. "Thank you, sir. I will go down to the kitchen and get the queen's tray and be right back." She moved swiftly by Efrian, opened the door, and facing the hallway, added, "And, sir, I will take this meeting with me into my passing."

***

The Erlking walked among his villagers, a smile peeking from under his mask. His thoughts were on the loyal, clean, full-blooded fae and their families that surrounded him. His chest widened with each intake of his breath as fae bowed as he passed. He paused before a small robin-egg colored cottage where a young boy sat in a grassy area near stone steps as his mother pulled peas from their shells.

"What are you building, young man?" the Erlking asked.

"A trap for the fire bugs, sir. Then I will put them in a bubble in my room at night."

"Are you not afraid they will die in your bubble?" Nereus asked the boy.

"No, sir," the child said. "There will be more tomorrow night."

"Clever boy," Nereus said, eyes twinkling above a hidden grin. "One day you will make a good guardsman like your father."

The boy jumped to his feet and ran toward the Erlking. "Is my father with you?" he asked, looking down the row of guards behind Nereus. "I don't see him, sir. Can you—"

"Jaris!" Efrian's mother stood so swiftly she tipped the bowl of peas. "You never address the Erlking like that without his request to do so!" Her face was bright red. "I am sorry, Your Highness. Please forgive him. He knows not what he's done."

"But Mama," Jaris said, "he talked to me first. It would be disrespectful to ignore our Erlking!"

Nereus watched the peas roll down the steps as his belly bounced with his laughter. "It is fine, my lady. Your child's question is well received and deserves an answer, Jynifer." The Erlking turned to the child. "Alas, Jaris, you are correct, your father is not with us. I have a mission for my Head Guard tonight and I wanted him well rested."

Jaris beamed with pleasure before bowing his head. "I am proud my father is in your service, sir."

Nereus bent and shook the young faeling's hand. "And I am blessed to have him."

***

"And you are sure Saul is the only guard at the entrance?"

"Yes. But only during the day. The entrance above is locked at night and only the Erlking has a key." Ova's cheeks turned pink and her hands tightened on the tray of soup and a crust of bread she carried. "He and I have...well, we are—"

"Never mind." Efrian waved her words off with a swing of his hand. "I understand," he said, and mentally chided himself for not going with his gut reaction earlier. "Still, he mustn't know that I am with you today, or why. It would force him to make judgment and put him in more danger."

Ova nodded and they continued silently down a circle staircase in a part of the castle he'd never been. Ova stopped several steps from a small platform below with a partial view of a wooden door. Efrian looked over the edge of the railing. A metal gate at the opposite side of the platform and wooden door was open. Stone stairs circled further below the platform and faded into darkness.

"That's Saul's quarters. Wait here, back against the wall, and away from the door's view. Saul always steps out and watches me go below until the candles no longer light my view. He is always there when I come back up...and we usually...chat a bit." Ova turned a flushed face from Efrian's view. "So, I will have to be very careful if you wish me to warn the queen of your impending arrival and her escape."

"Best to say nothing." Efrian leaned back to look above them. "I wish we could fly out the arrowslit we passed outside the stairwell, but I'm sure it's magicked like the rest of the castle's unguarded exits. Never mind. I have another idea."

"It's not magicked," Ova said.

Efrian abruptly turned to Ova and didn't hide his surprise. "How do you know this?"

"I've used it many times to visit at night. There is a door in the kitchen that is not magicked. It leads to gated compost piles. It's used often day and night to discard kitchen waste. There is also a rope guided shoot in the kitchen that is not magicked. It has openings on two floors above. The staff used it before the rebellion to deliver and gather guests trays. One opening is down the hall from the guest quarters, and the other is near the Erlking's chambers."

"Excellent," Efrian said as Ova pointed at the wall; a reminder for him to hide from view. He took one last look below and said, "When you come back up, I will need you to keep him busy while I escape with the queen."

"It will be my pleasure, sir!" Ova said as she stepped further down the stairs.

"I'm sure it will," Efrian mumbled, the corners of his mouth turned slightly upward, as

Efrian backed out of view and wondered what other atrocities lie hidden below.

***

"We need to get you a bath and some clean clothes." A smile lit Reka's face as she and

Coralina slowly helped Mabyn across long dried grass and toward one of the wagons.

"How did Efrian find us?" Coralina asked.

The queen gave both friends a weak smile. Each had one arm and were almost carrying her. "Holding me in his arms as if I were precious cargo, he flew over the Bad Lands until we saw the light from your camp."

"Well, crap," Coralina said. "Another thing to worry about."

"How could that be?" Reka asked. "I remember asking Ozil if we could fly over the Bad Lands to search for fae that had escaped the Erlking's wrath. He said they had tried many times but the Bad Lands was covered with a thick haze. He even had guards patrolling for escapees that might try to get back over the fence. That we would see, but never found a one."

"No wonder Nereus laughed when stating no one is capable of escaping penalties," Reka said, "not even with their stupid attempts."

"I'm sure he felt they were devoured by the dark creatures that dwell here," Mabyn said.

Coralina and Reka shared a look over Mabyn's head.

"You don't have to hide your thoughts, ladies," Mabyn said. "And I'd prefer you to share the hatred you have for my husband that I have." She lifted her head as they approached the wagon and tsked at Ozil, wings buzzing, as he hovered beside the entrance. "You could've at least let me bathe before greeting me, Captain Ozil."

"The devil be damned," Ozil said over a smile. "There is no shame in your appearance, Queen Mabyn. I see only the gift of survival in your soul. You wear that well."

"Sorrowfully so," Mabyn said. "Let us hope Efrian made it back before Nereus so we can share in his safe reprise."

CHAPTER TEN

Among the Falling Leaves

A brown leaf tumbled from the tree, pulled from its perch in the light breeze. It landed at Coralina's feet, piled upon countless others. The black sky, usually blocked from view by the thick canopy, shined through the thinning tree branches. She picked up the leaf, the size of her, and examined it. Its gold color had completely drained away, along with every drop of water within. Coralina twisted it gently, but even the simple motion was enough to split the dry plant. She held it up to her face and peeked through the hole to see Rampart walking toward her.

"Even among all these dying trees," she said behind the leaf, "your expression is somehow the bleakest thing I see."

Rampart's head hung. "Yeah, well... just weary I suppose. And tired of trying to hide it from the troops. It can be exhausting pretending to be positive all the time."

Coralina dropped the leaf. "I understand that, but at least we can complain to each other." She gave a supportive smile. "How is Queen M doing?"

"Resting, semi-comfortably," Rampart said. "It could be a while before Reka's at full strength. But she'll also get there."

Coralina's eyes dropped. "Sometimes I wonder what was worse, being hunted by Nereus or held hostage to his whims. At least we can fight back; Queen Mabyn had to sit in her tower, so close to her people but never allowed to engage."

Rampart shrugged. "Can't say either of those two options are all that appealing to me."

"Fair enough." She laughed. Spinning on the balls of her feet, Coralina turned her back to him and walked to the large tree ahead of her. She placed a delicate hand on the dry bark peeling from the trunk. "Any news from the scouts?"

Rampart took a deep breath and held it for a moment, a sign Coralina knew signaled bad news. "Yes. They returned not too long ago," he said. "Gillmog pond was bled dry, just like all the others."

"Told you it would be," she said. "That's two trail rations you owe me."

Rampart sighed. "I honestly didn't think the Erlking's magic could reach that far."

Coralina scoffed. "The man might be an arrogant, cruel bastard, but there's no doubt he's a powerful one. We'll be fine, though; there's plenty of water at camp. If we ration it, we should have enough for a few months."

"That's not the point, Cor," Rampart said, his footsteps crunching on dry leaves as he walked closer. "Look around. This is happening everywhere. The forest is dying. If we can't return the water to its roots soon, there won't be anything left to save."

"I'm aware, Rampart," Coralina said sharply and spun to meet his eyes. "You think I don't know that!"

Rampart's expression dropped like a scolded dog. "This war must end, one way or another. Nereus has lost it, slaughtering villages, drying the lands. He'll turn everything and everyone to dust if this continues."

"Yeah, I know that, too," Coralina grumbled. "He's trying to force us into attacking. The problem is, I think it's going to work." She paced, eyes glued to the ground. "We know he's willing to let the land rot, and he knows we aren't. That puts the pressure on us. Now all he has to do is batten down the hatches and wait for us to walk into the teeth of his army."

Rampart crossed his arms. "Going out in a blaze of glory, huh?"

The words struck Coralina like a lightning bolt. "You don't think we can win?"

"Do you? We've fought in the hills, valleys, hell, even in the air, but never even tried to approach the castle. We both know why that is; we don't have the strength in our army for that kind of frontal assault."

Coralina locked eyes with him. "I'm not planning some suicide mission. If we march on the capital it's with the intent of taking it."

Rampart matched her glare. "How do you plan to do that?"

A gust of wind swirled through the trees, rustling the dry leaves and tearing them from the trees. Rampart's question weighed heavy on her chest. She didn't have a good answer for him. Scenarios of attacking the castle had played through her mind frequently over the years, but they'd all ended the same, with the rebellions' bodies littering the grounds. Even with the determination they had, the numbers game would always play against them. The burning of Copper Groves showed that. The Erlking's guard stormed through like a wave of armor and swords, showing what the full might of their army could do.

And yet, Coralina meant what she said, and believed it. If she brought the rebels to the castle gates, she fully intended to take the throne from Nereus. The how was a mystery to even herself, but somehow, she knew it was possible.

"I'm working on it," she finally said. "But I don't want you talking to the troops like we're marching them toward their doom. When everyone is rested, we'll start heading toward the capital. We'll gather as much support as we can along the way. With the queen on our side, others will join. She'll be able to confirm everything we've been saying about the Erlking, about his hatred, the slaughters, and they won't be able to deny it. With the forest dying around them more will be ready to act against the crown."

Rampart nodded. "You're probably right, but there's still a major power we could use that we're not." He stepped toward her. "I think it's time we talk to Aldul again, see if the jinn are willing to send more support."

"No. I told you; I'm not going to gain the throne by aligning myself with the jinn. That's exactly what Nereus did, and I won't be anything like my father."

Rampart gently grasped her forearms. "I think you're looking at this the wrong way, Cor. Think of it this way, Nereus used his alliance with Talock to take over the lands and impose their own prejudice upon the people. Everything they imposed was put in place to separate the people, divide them, keep them from becoming a threat to them or their rule. What you're aiming to do is the complete opposite. You want to align with the jinn not for the purpose of your own well-being, but for the better of the people."

Coralina stifled a smile. His gentle touch sparked a shiver that radiated from her arms down her spine. She was sure he felt it, but she still refused to acknowledge it. "But how is it going to look to the other clans? I'm trying to gain trust from the people. Why should they think I'm any different from Nereus? They don't personally know me. After everything that's happened, how could they?"

Rampart hinted a smile. "Well, hate to put too fine of a point on it, but it's not like you could be a whole lot worse than him."

Coralina laughed. "Wow, thanks."

He tapped her elbow with his pointer finger. "But really, think about it. The Erlking's men don't follow him because they like him. It's just that they're too afraid to cross his path. At least you can give them a chance for a difference; sometimes that can be enough. And don't forget, it's not just the support of the jinn you have, but you have their Queen, Mabyn, and a freaking angel on your side as well. You're finding supporters and uniting races where Nereus could only drive them apart. That has to count for something, right?"

Coralina could see the logic in what Rampart was saying, but still hesitation lingered. She began to wonder if it was because she honestly thought the people would reject the alliance, or because of her own distrust of the jinn. That thought brought a pang of guilt. "Alright," she said. "I'll talk with Aldul when he returns. It's hard to say how much the jinn will support, but if I can convince them Nereus is still implementing the ban—which he is—maybe they'll be willing to help."

"Well, you know Aldul will push for it," Rampart said. "Doubt they want to have a full-scale war on their hands, but after what happened with him and the Erlking at the castle, they might not have a choice but to help remove Nereus. It's not like he's going to forget Aldul helped free a couple of his prized prisoners."

"Yeah, and he's not known for his ability to forgive and forget, either." Thoughts of the recently slaughtered villagers flashed before her eyes. She pulled away from Rampart and crossed her arms. "I'm going to talk with Cal, too. He's the only half fae that has been able to transform and use his full power. I know his case is pretty unique, but I still wonder if he'd have some ideas on how to get the others to use their full potential."

Rampart folded his leathery wings behind him. "Sure, why not. Worth a try at least. Even if nothing comes of it, it'll give them more training time." He sighed. "Now all we have to do is figure a way to get the army through the town surrounding the capital, infiltrate the castle, and then take down one of the most powerful water fae alive. Can't be too hard."

Coralina watched another leaf tumble from the tree; it swayed back and forth in the wind, in a way that reminded her of the dances wind fae performed. It'd been so long since she'd seen them. "Rampart, I'm going to ask you to do something." Her eyes locked on his. "Note, I said ASK. I won't command you to do this, and I want it to be clear if you say no, I won't tell anyone you refused."

Rampart smiled slyly with the corner of his mouth. "Wow, asking huh? Never thought I'd see the day."

"I'm serious. There's no shame in saying no."

"For the love of... just tell me what you're thinking, Cor."

She felt the saliva dry in her mouth. "I wanted...was hoping you and Dusk could ride ahead of the caravan. While we try to gather supplies, you could talk to the citizens in the town around the castle. Since Nereus pulled as many of the clans there as he could, it'd be very hard to get through there without some sort of support from the fae. Maybe they'd even be able to give us information about weak spots for the Guard."

The air stilled around them. At first, Coralina thought it was a lull in the breeze, then she realized she was instinctively using her powers to hold the air in place like others would hold their breaths. She slowly released it and hoped Rampart wouldn't notice.

Rampart nodded thoughtfully. The playful smile disappeared. "One of the leaders of the rebels jumping straight into the heart of the Erlking's guard. Yeah, that's pretty risky."

"Obviously, you'd need to wear some other clothing to help conceal yourself," she said. "But I know you're good at glamour spells, probably the best I've ever seen. If anyone could sneak through the capital without getting caught, it'd be you. But like I said, it's only a volunteering mission. It's dangerous, and if you get caught..." Her words got caught in her throat. "There won't be much we'll be able to do to help. You'll be on your own."

Rampart examined her for a moment before stepping sideways, his expression lost in thought. "Makes sense. I'm sure there are a lot of the clans that are angry from being brought there from their homelands. If word spread around the town, we could find a whole army waiting for us." He laughed. "Hell, maybe by the time you get there I'll already have killed Nereus and taken the throne. You'll have to be nice to me if you want me to get up from it."

"Rampart..."

"No, it's a good call, and could be the final nail in Nereus's coffin. And like you said, I'd be the best person to do it," Rampart said. "Ozil would stand out like a sore thumb and he's awful with disguise spells, Reka has too much heat on her since her escape, and you are needed here with the troops to prepare them for battle. Really, I'm the only one who can go."

Coralina felt hollow inside, as if suddenly she was full of nothing but air. "I was hoping you'd say no," she said softly.

"But it's the right call, and I'm glad you made it." His expression was determined, then softened with a mischievous grin. "Plus, I look forward to telling Dusk about where we're going. He's going to be thrilled."

Coralina laughed. "Yeah, when we meet up, he'll probably try to kill me." She took a breath and pursed her lips. "Just, try to make sure we meet up again, okay?"

Rampart smiled. "Yeah, no problem. I'll get the clans riled up for ya, and I'll be waiting for everyone when you get there." The two locked eyes one last time, before Rampart nodded awkwardly. "Well, I guess... good luck," he said. "I'll be seeing you soon."

Coralina looked for the right words. "Yeah, you bet," she choked out just before the silence became uncomfortable.

She watched him turn and head back toward camp.

"'You bet,'" she grumbled under her breath. "Why is that man both the easiest person to talk to, but also the hardest?"

CHAPTER ELEVEN

Wind Wails Down Halls, Seeps Into Walls, and Slowly the Castle Begins to Fall

Efrian zipped back through the arrowslit Queen Mabyn's chambermaid had made him aware of, and effortlessly returned to his post to find the Erlking in a cheerful mood.

"Ah, Efrian, your wife, Jynifer, is lovely. Very respectful. And your boy, Jaris, why, his inquisitive nature is entertaining and speaks loudly for his intelligence. With minor adjustments to that strong-willed disposition of his, I'm sure Jaris will make as loyal a guardsman as his father. You must be proud."

Efrian forced a smile. "Thank you, Sir. Coming from you, that's an honorable complement."

Nereus slapped Efrian on the back. "Come, share a cup of port with me. I want to brief you on the villages forming around the castle."

The room was well-lit with magicked lanterns. Four were extravagantly gilded over a leafy pattern and hung between red velvet drapes. If the drapes were closed it shut out a view of the villages and the atrocities below. Efrian knew the staff closed drapes when cleaning the Erlking's quarters, and even then, only when the Erlking was not in the castle. They did this to avoid the dark gardens in the courtyard below where poles pushed into the ground held the bodies of their kinsmen. Not even Faery Land's most carnivorous creatures attempted to pull the flesh off their bones. That left the feast to a murder of crows circling daily, and guardsmen armed with bows and arrows to keep them away.

Such an appropriate color, red. Efrian sighed as he removed his eyes from the curtains. The scaffolding in front of the drapes and across the length of the entire back wall made it difficult to pull one of the many indoor evils from his mind. For many hours Efrian had been forced to watch the Erlking walk the platform, pausing before each arrow slit above the windows as though examining works of art. He dared not remove his eyes from Nereus while being forced to take in the man's sickness.

Efrian swallowed bile threatening his taste buds. His insides rankled while Nereus pulled two small tankards from a tallboy and set them on a small table where he took his private meals.

Pouring a dark golden liquid from a decanter into the tankards, Nereus said, "Our day is coming close, my friend. When the villages are all demolished and rebuilt here, the rest of the lands will wither and die, expanding like the Bad Lands I created so long ago. That will increase the deadly fear of exile. I encouraged those down under to seek refuge and food in the Bad Lands. In turn, they stay away from Faery Land."

The Erlking extended a tankard toward Efrian and smiled when he took it. "Unlike my guardsmen, the fae having lost their self-built towns are now becoming even more fearful of the rapidly expanding darkness. It tickles me." Nereus chuckled and lifted his bejeweled tankard. "My self-made forest surrounding the castle will become filled with more creatures from the pits of Hell. My people will not escape the new world I am creating, and those from other lands thinking to save them will not cross the darkness.

"There will be no more half-bred fae in my world, Efrian. We will once again be the fae humans read about in myths and legends. We will multiply and prosper and then I will begin to expand our territory a little at a time. I will never again allow my race to be tainted. That will discourage my villagers from straying the protection of the castle and guardsmen."

And live in constant fear of becoming a victim of your excruciatingly painful and deadly spontaneity.

"Let us drink to a new, pure, and powerful Faery Lands and those who would be crazy enough to build camps among night creatures that thrive on the death of others."

The tankards clinked and sloshed port over Efrian's fingers as Nereus took a hefty swig. Efrian hesitantly pulled the cup to his mouth and barely let the port touch his lips. He rebuked the toast with a silent oath to make sure the Erlking's wishes would become the death of him.

Nereus studied his head guardsman as Efrian studied a fire popping behind a rock hearth out of the other Fae's view.

"I am weary from my walk today," Nereus suddenly said. "Have a plate of food brought up to my room in an hour, Guardsman, and then see that I am not disturbed until dusk." Over his leather mask, the Erlking's eyes studied Efrian's expression. "I want to visit the cells below the castle when I wake. And you will accompany me. It's time I respect your endless loyalty and extend your knowledge."

Efrian felt a roiling madness in the Erlking's words and tightened his grip on the tankard as Nereus waved him away. "Make your rounds of the castle staff. I want to know if their employment warrants the wages I pay them. You can fill me in tonight during out trip downward."

"As you wish, Your Highness," Efrian said, and set his drink down. Head bowed, he stepped backward toward the door to exit the Erlking's chambers.

Nereus's laugh was overexcited. "You can finish your drink before you leave, my friend." Nereus walked through an arch leading into his bed chamber. "I want to get out of these dusty clothes and bathe before dinner."

***

Efrian wandered the castle making his way to the kitchen and Ova, Queen Mabyn's chambermaid. With each fae he encountered, the desire to warn of this night's upcoming doom when Nereus found his wife no longer in the cell below grew. However, he knew for sure that only two knew of Queen Mabyn's imprisonment below. If he did warn others, the news would spread swiftly. Tonight, Nereus would no doubt, immediately, begin interrogations. A warning to the staff now would only increase the Erlking's ability to doubt their innocence.

Efrian knew he himself would be a captive party to all of this and feared for his own loyalty to be judged. Had Nereus already tested his loyalty by telling him he would accompany him below tonight? Were the Erlking's eyes judging? His smile condescending, deliberating, probing? Chills ran through Efrian's body as his mind ran visuals of the conversation in the Erlking's chambers.

What was on my mind during the conversation? Fear? Shame? Guilt? No, I had only felt a strong desire to attend to the staff. Surely that could have only been determined as obedience. I was ordered to see that the staff had been doing their jobs. Wasn't that what Nereus wanted me to feel, the strength to administer his wishes properly?

Efrain didn't need to bet his life that everyone would be questioned throughout the night, including him. Although his hatred for the Erlking was always well hidden, it was as hard to keep spontaneous reactions from Nereus as it was artless untruths. His ability to sense subterfuge was impeccable. But Efrian worried more for the maid and guard than himself.

It is my turn to scrutinize Nereus, not the opposite, and it's my responsibility to figure out how to save the innocents that will pay for what I did; I must plan what to do next.

Efrian walked the upper and mid-levels of the castle and spoke with the staff still completing late afternoon duties. All were told the Erlking sent him to see if his orders were properly being taken care of. It was not long before Efrian was hurrying through the remaining drafty halls and poorly lit castle staircases toward the kitchen where most of the staff would be preparing for the evening and late-night duties. Ova's safety was heavy on his mind. So was his family.

Efrian always knew he would have to move his family far away from the castle eventually. Today, there was still time to warn Queen Mabyn's chambermaid, and a guard that had no knowledge of what he had helped accomplish, to leave the castle at once. Tonight, he needed to be by the Erlking's side, hiding the anger, swallowing the disgust, and accepting of the tortures ahead.

Efrian strongly felt the Erlking would not harm him or his family tonight. Nereus would be deflecting anger and threats on his staff, and later the villagers until he had no one left but Efrian. *Yes, the Erlking's madness will stay within the walls of his castle.* His immediate and unthinkable cruelties would be on those he felt should have known how and when his Queen had achieved her freedom and who he felt had kept it from him.

Although Efrian knew Ova understood the ramifications of abusing her loyalty to the Erlking, without his persistence, she would have remained dutiful and, in turn, safe. She was doomed if he could not convince her to leave immediately.

***

"The Erlking wishes an early evening meal before he naps," Efrian said as he stood in the castle kitchen. "He will take it in his chambers." All eyes in the kitchen locked on the tall, muscular Head Guardsman as he spoke.

"Has the huntsman brought in a fresh kill today, Vonda?" Efrian asked the head cook.

"Yes, Sir," the stout woman said, head bowed, shoulders rising as she spoke.

"Well, speak up, woman. What beast was it today?"

"Wild boar, Sir." A dribble of sweat rolled between her brows, slid down the side of Vonda's nose, and fell to darken the floor, a dime size circle, between her shoes. Scraggly gray hair, wispy as a spiderweb, had escaped from a white cap on her head and clung to the faery's temples and neck.

"Excellent." Efrian smiled. "Gamey, just the way our Erlking likes it. Cook a hefty slice over the fire and dress it with berries. Make sure the bread is warm from the oven and throw that mint sauce you are so famous for over the meat."

Vonda chuckled. "Yes, Sir! I just made some up this morning."

"Excellent!"

The urge to warn the staff was strong, but Efrian's eyes strayed from their faces and took in the kitchen around him. "The Erlking asked I make rounds of the castle and staff. We all know what that means."

Vonda moved her weight from one leg to the other. "Does he plan a visit?"

"No one ever knows for sure, Vonda," said one of the male fae.

Efrian nodded in agreement. "Make this kitchen and the help sparkle with orderly cleanliness in the happenstance our Erlking elects to make a tour."

"Don't stand there eyeing at him," Vonda said to the male fae. "Get a move on!"

The atmosphere in the kitchen went from anxious to earnest as smiles spread and action commenced. Efrian's eyes captured Ova's with a request as he crossed the kitchen and stepped through a door, kicking up a cloud of dusty dry dirt as he walked away.

Before the kitchen door swung shut, Efrian heard Ova. "I'll get the bucket, Miss Vonda," she said. "Looks like it needs emptying."

"Thank you, Ova, and hurry back. There's much to be done."

"Yes, Ma'am," Ova said, and the door shut out the noise of hustle and bustle within the kitchen.

Ova rounded the corner and smiled at Efrian standing near a wooden pig bin. "He's going down to the cells tonight, isn't he?" she asked, and dumped the bucket of slop into the trough.

"Yes," Efrian answered.

"It's not like we didn't know this was comin', Sir," Ova said. Her fingers shook and her knuckles turned white as her hands gripped the handle of the bucket.

"I'm sorry," Efrian said.

"Don't be," Ova said. "I do not regret what I did, any more than my Saul will when he finds out I helped. We talked of an escape for our queen many times, Sir."

Efrian's slow intake of breath caused Ova to raise a hand. "Don't you go feeling guilty, now."

"I had as much a part in this as you," Efrian said. "Unfortunately, I must stay. But you do not have to. Take Saul out of here tonight before Nereus gets down to the cell. Go through the arrow slit you mentioned was not magicked. Don't let anybody see you both leave. My warning is for your ears only until you get out of range of the castle. I'm sure the dead will shiver in their graves tonight, and no rock will be left unturned."

"We also thought about how we would get away. What good would it do? Where would we go?" Ova lowered her head. "You know he will find us and the punishment will be much worse than a shared cup of tea laced with Foxglove. That is what we planned to do, and then lay on his bed until our hearts stop beating."

Efrian swallowed hard as his eyes scanned the yard. They were alone. But that wasn't where his mind had wandered. What he was thinking chilled him to the bone. He put his hand over hers.

"Do you know where my cottage is in the village?"

"Yes," Ova said. "But—"

"Go there," Efrian said before he could change his mind. "We have a root closet in the cellar. Tell my wife everything. Tell her I will hopefully be joining you tonight or in the early morning shade." He paused, squeezed Ova's hands, and watched her choke back a rebuttal. "It is going to be a long night, and the Erlking asked me to accompany him. If he senses I am a part of this..." Efrian avoided Ova's gaze and tightened his lips.

"And if you don't show up before morning?"

"Take my family and fly over the Bad Lands until you find the others." Efrian couldn't take his words back. Instead, he nailed down their need to leave. "Because if I don't arrive, it will be my family the Erlking kills first. Do you understand?"

"Yes," Ova said as tears ran down her cheeks. "May the magic of our kind be with you, Efrian."

He let go of her hands. "And with you, Saul, and my family as well." Efrian turned to the fields where his guards slept. "Wipe those tears away before you return to the kitchen, and don't wait long after dark to leave." His wings spread and he took flight.

Ova wiped her face with a soiled apron and turned back to the castle with a feeling she was surprised she had. Relief.

***

"Mabyn has always been my worst follower," Nereus said, and locked eyes with Efrian. "She has held back love and respect for many years, and near the end she threatened to leave the castle, a cohort for the fae that had caused the destruction on our lands. She needed to die a horrible death, but instead I let her live."

For the first time, Nereus was not wearing his mask in Efrian's presence. The scares on his face pulsed streams of light with his angry words. It was hard for Efrian to look at but he nodded an understanding in the Erlking's direction as they moved through the halls. Efrian knew where Nereus was going with the conversation. The Erlking's words were more horrific than the scars on his face.

Mabyn is not the problem. She was never the problem.

"She refused me her body *and* her loyalty, threatened me. I...I..." Nereus silenced the beat of their steps on the stairwell by abruptly turning his body to look directly into Efrian's eyes. "...imprisoned her below."

In that paused moment, Efrian struggled with a respectful and supportive expression, but behind his eyes raced a need to put the fae down then and there. He knew he could not end the Erlking's life alone; it would be a sure death to try. "What are we going to do with her, my Erlking?"

Nereus's lips curled and he snickered. "We...aren't going to do anything at the moment. It gives me piece of mind to watch her suffer for her sins against me. I only visit her tonight because I have decided to trust you with her confinement."

"Your faith in me swells my chest with pride, Sir." Efrian pushed the words out of his mouth, and he mentally begged he needn't say more for the moment.

Nereus patted his shoulder and started down the stairs again. As they rounded the corner to take the path that led to the guardsman's post, Efrian silently pled they did not stop at the door. He held his breath as they passed.

Nereus pointed over his shoulder and at the door. "The guardsman, a fine fellow and from what I hear, has a liking to my Mabyn's head servant." He chuckled at the thought. "Ah, the wildly ways of a female in heat can craze the brain of a good man, don't you agree, my friend?"

"I do, Sir," Efrian said and forced a smile. "I know that feeling only too well." It sickened him to speak of his wife in a worldly way, but the smile he forced came from the love he felt for her.

The Erlking burst with laughter. "But in your case this is a good thing. A clean thing. You are both full blooded and worked hard to propagate our lands. Your son is a fine example of this."

Efrian found it easy to mentally agree while his gut pained him. But found moving his thoughts in a direction he wished his expression to follow seemed to work. *Maybe if I think of the hundreds of fae carcasses hanging from polls in our courtyard when he sees Mabyn is missing, I can feel the level of anger I need to make it through the rest of the night with my head still attached to my shoulders.*

CHAPTER TWELVE

Breakthrough

The high sun beat down on the rebel camp. The fae, used to the protection of the trees, hung their heads in the radiating heat. Only a few brown leaves defiantly hung from the branches now, clinging on with withered stems, stubbornly refusing to let go. Coralina couldn't help but feel they were a good representation of the rebellion; dry, dying, but too stubborn to give up. Either future generations would look at them as resilient and uncompromising in their pursuit of justice, or fools slamming their bodies against the impenetrable wall of the guard. That, of course, completely depended on who won.

Aoife stood in front of Coralina, her eyes closed and breathing slow and steady. Coralina gave the rest of the half fae time off. Working with a large group of them was proving frustrating, especially with Broka's constant whining. Out of all of them, Aoife was the most enthusiastic to unlock her full power. "I think I can feel a difference between the pixie energy and the Fae," Aoife said, her forehead wrinkled. "It's there, but I can't really focus on it. Kind of like those floaty things that get in your eye. As soon as I try to focus, it just slips away."

"Don't fight it," Coralina said. "Just try to get a feel for it, get familiar with how it's different from your fae side."

Aoife smiled; her glittery cheeks sparkled in the sun. "It feels warm, and bright, like a sunbeam. The fae side is more like a strong wind, chaotic and unrelenting."

Coralina crossed her arms. "That's good. Now try to calm the fae side. Push through and try to bring the Pixie forward."

Aoife's lips thinned as she concentrated. Her pink hue grew darker and eyes darted underneath closed lids. At last, she let out a long-held breath in a huff. "Damn it, I lost it. Now it's buried underneath the fae power again."

Coralina sighed. It was disappointing but expected. Still, it was further than they'd gotten on previous tries. "Alright, let's take a break."

"But I can do it!" Aoife reached her delicate hands forward. "It was right at my fingertips; I just couldn't grab it."

"You made a lot of progress," Coralina said, in a comforting voice that she was still getting used to. "You got closer than the others have. Let's call that a win for now, take a breather, and when we come back, we'll work on your breathing. Can't have you pass out while you're focusing."

Aoife grunted. "Fine. I'll get some water. I'll be back in ten minutes so we can continue." She turned on her heels and hurried off to camp.

Coralina smiled. The half pixie impressed her more and more every day. The more trials they'd gone through, the more tenacious and stubborn she became. When Aoife first joined the rebels she was quiet and meek, using her small stature to stay unnoticed. Now she brazenly challenged anyone she disagreed with.

And Coralina loved it.

It was an attitude she wished would ripple through the camp. As Coralina looked around, she saw many half fae with their heads down and wings dropped on their shoulders. A few roamed around with shuffled feet, picking up dry leaves off the ground that could be turned into carrying bags, patches for the wagons, or even clothing. Others practiced combat stances or worked on fortifying their armor. They still carried on with their tasks, but the enthusiasm drained away just as the water was drained from the forest.

Coralina sighed and tilted her head up, letting the sunbeams hit her face. She almost didn't hear Cal approach.

"Still no luck with the transformation, huh?" he asked.

Coralina fought back the urge to snap at him. She had promised herself she would try to be more diplomatic, but when people asked questions they knew the answer to, it always poked at her nerves. "No," she answered calmly. "But it was a good session. She managed to find a way to tell her two energies apart. She just can't separate them yet."

Cal kicked at the dirt. "Well, that's actually pretty incredible. When you've lived with both sides intertwined, separating them is like pulling flour out of a cake after it's been baked."

Coralina looked at him. "You managed to do it."

"That's different. I was trying to bring my fae side to the surface. Basically the opposite of what they're trying to do. And don't forget, I can only transform like that here, where the fae energy is most prominent." Cal smiled. "Also, you helped."

"Heh, yeah sure I did," she scoffed. "I mostly just teased you."

Cal shrugged. "Still helped me figure out the missing pieces to the puzzle. Like it or not, you're taking some credit for it."

"Alright, enough of your flattery bullshit," Coralina chortled. "Doesn't really matter if I gave you a step-by-step presentation on how to do it. The point is, right now, I'm failing. That's all that matters."

Cal arched an eyebrow. "You are? Oh, I didn't realize." He looked around the camp. "Guess I was confused because I see a large group of fae following and trying their best to support you. Don't usually see that with people who are failing."

Coralina stared at him with a blank face. "Does your cheerleader routine have an off switch?"

Cal laughed. "Well, I am an angel you know. Kind of in our DNA. But I'll try to tone it down if you'd like." His eyes scanned the camp. "Point is, we're not done yet. We've pulled off some great underdog victories before, and we can do it again."

Coralina sat cross legged on the ground. "I don't get it, though. How were you able to transform so easily into your half fae form?"

Cal shook his head. "Easy my ass. It took Nereus admitting he killed my mother, and a touch of murderous rage, to bring it out of me. And the fae energy draws on that side down here."

Coralina sighed. "Great, then all we need to do is draw out specific energy from countless worlds for a large variety of half fae. Sounds easy, doesn't it?" She rubbed her knees in frustration; somehow, she found the hot friction calming. "Maybe that's why we've had no luck. I've been training everyone at once, but they're all from different backgrounds, different lands. Of course it's not going to be the same for them."

Coralina felt her mind spinning. She knew there was no way she'd have time for everyone individually, even if that would work. She began to wonder if it would be best to scrap the whole training all together. Soon, the final attack on the castle would be taking place, and she didn't want to wear out her troops training. But without their special powers, would they even stand a chance? She didn't know.

Then, a thought occurred. She eyed Cal standing next to her. In keeping with the fae way, if there wasn't enough time to train them properly, maybe there was a way they could cheat.

Cal met her gaze and frowned. "Why are you looking at me like that? Should I be worried?"

"You have healing abilities, right?" she asked.

"Yeah, of course. You've seen me use them before."

"How do they work?"

Cal scoffed. "I don't remember exactly; it was so long ago I was taught it's basically just muscle memory for me now."

Coralina stood. "I've known a few healers in my time. One of them described it to me as manipulating the person's life force, molding it to concentrate on the areas that needed healing."

Cal nodded. "Yeah, that sounds right. What of it?"

Coralina smacked his arm. "Manipulating energies, Cal. Doesn't that sound like exactly what we've been trying to teach the half fae to do?"

Cal raised his hand. "Hold on, before you get too excited, what you're talking about is beyond what I can do. You're talking pinpoint surgical manipulation; I just bombard the person and hope for the best."

"Maybe that's enough. Hold on, I want to try something." She turned to the camp. "Aoife, come here."

Aoife, who sipped water from a ladle made from a whirligig seed, quickly hurried over. "Ready to start again?" she asked, taking one last sip before dropping the ladle.

"Yes," Coralina said. "Do you think you can get to the point where you can feel your pixie side?"

Aoife smiled. "Yeah! Now that I know what it feels like, that part is easy. Just not sure where to go from there."

"I think we might be able to help you a bit with that." Coralina turned to Cal. "When she gets to that point, I'll have you heal her."

Aoife tilted her head. "But... I'm not injured."

"Yeah I know," Coralina said. "I just want to see what happens. Are you ready?"

Aoife nodded, and shut her eyes. Her breathing slowed and her jaw clinched. After a minute, she smiled. "There, got it, what now?"

Coralina nodded to Cal, and he stepped next to Aoife. He gently placed a hand on her back, and a light glow emanated from her. Aoife took a deep breath in, as if someone slashed her with cold water.

"Whoa!" she exclaimed. "Everything just lit up like a pack of glow worms in the night. Wow, it's beautiful."

Coralina smiled. It was exactly what she hoped for. But she still tried to keep her excitement hampered. "Great! You think you can pull your pixie side out now?"

Aoife's eyes danced beneath their lids. "You know what, I think I might. It's all so clear now. Let me see if I can focus on it. Just a sec."

Aoife's face scrunched as the vein in her temple bulged and turned her pink skin purple. The glow around her intensified and turned pink. Cal stepped away from her. After seconds that felt like minutes, Aoife smiled. "There, I got it."

The glitter on the pixie's cheeks spread through her whole body. Even her hair developed a shine. The ground beneath her rumbled. Blades of grass sprouted at her feet and wound around her, hoisting her into the air as they grew. Her eyes snapped open with glowing purple irises. "I can feel it. The pixie side is so beautiful. It's so in touch with life and nature. It's amazing!"

The other half fae around the camp dropped what they were doing and rushed over. "Holy shit, Aoife did it!" Broca shouted.

Coralina felt a wave of elation course through her. For a moment, she felt she glowed just like Aoife did. This breakthrough could turn the tides in a fight with the guard. There was still a lot to do before the rest were ready, but today proved one thing. It was possible, and for now, that was all Coralina needed to know.

CHAPTER THIRTEEN

A Rain of Terror

"Who would be fearless enough to free Mabyn?" Nereus bellowed. "I swear on the helplessness of our unborn changelings, I will find them and show them what fear is. I'll pluck their wings, pull out their hearts, and crush their helpless bodies under my feet! Mabyn is dead when I catch up with her! And I will, for the love of my throne and my people, I swear I will find her. Those who freed her will watch me slowly torture Mabyn for hours, maybe days! Yes, days. All the while knowing they will suffer the same death, half-starved and weak from hanging on the poles in the courtyard. Because I will announce from the beginning that anyone that took part in the queen's disappearance physically, mentally, or with words of encouragement, will suffer the same death."

The Erlking paced the empty cell, stomping the fetid soil into clouds circling his bare ankles. The black slippers he wore, trimmed in gold, were dusted like garish Petit Fours with the foul-smelling dirt.

Nereus ground his teeth and grumbled. "Efrian, I find it hard to believe you neither perceived nor observed something of an odd nature during your rounds today. Think! Now that we know she escaped, there had to be something said or done to give you a clue."

"Nothing, my Erlking!" Efrian said. "And damn anyone you find to be part of this!"

Efrian already felt worn by the Erlking's interrogations, and the evening was young. His expressions had shifted from faked rage to a real fear for his family. Both had been a struggle mentally. He feared Nereus could read his mind, or at the very least, felt his hidden feelings. Directing mental reactions was much more difficult than the outward ones. Now, hiding a blanket of hope that covered relief for his family and their escape was difficult.

Efrian kept his eyes on the Erlking's feet as he himself held back from following the frenzied path Nereus took along the bars of the rank smelling cell.

Rubbing the stubble on his chin and finger combing hair from his face, Efrian repeatedly tried to calm frustrated intakes of breath that came automatically in situations like this, but it was becoming more difficult the longer he spent in the bowels of the castle alone with Nereus. His eyes jerked from the cell to the man in the leather face mask. Nereus was definitely escalating and the evening had barely begun.

As much as Efrian hated it, he needed to coax a departure. "My Erlking, might I suggest we go up and gather the castle staff. I directly spoke with so little of them as I thought I was on an average check of the premises duties with the staff." He blinked when Nereus stopped abruptly and turned to look directly at him. "Although, I must say," Efrian hurriedly alleged. "Even if I were assigned the task of finding the wrongdoers, I am not as gifted as you, Sir. I can only ask, but you feel their lies and truths."

"Guard!" Nereus yelled and shoved the cell door so hard, it bounced off the bars and forced Nereus to push it away again.

Efrian held back the fear rushing through his body searching for a place to escape.

"Let's get to the bottom of this!" Nereus stepped away from the cell and headed up the steps with Efrian close behind.

At the platform where Ova had looked up at him before entering the guard's room, Nereus pounded his fist on the door.

Efrian knew the guard was long gone and stood silently beside the Erlking.

"Wake up, you useless bastard," Nereus shouted. "You will pay dearly for this gaffe!"

Efrian mentally counted off seconds and then expelled a noisy breath after Nereus pulled open the door to find the small room empty.

The Erlking slowly and quietly turned away from the room. "And now we know who helped Mabyn, do we not?"

"We just might," Efrian said. He shook his head slowly and forced himself to bare teeth and growl. "Damn me to Hell! I did not speak with the fae this morning. I am shamed, my Erlking. I am at your mercy." Efrian bent to one knee and bowed. "I will not blame you for putting me to my death, right here."

Efrian cringed as he felt the Erlking's hand on his head.

"I have disappointed you, Nereus." Efrian's voice trembled. "I am unworthy of my title."

"Get up, Efrian." Nereus removed his hand and placed it under his headguard's arm. "You are worthy of your title. You did not order him to release Mabyn. You, as I, trusted him. We are both guilty."

Efrian stood, head still bowed. "Thank you, Sir."

"Look at me," Nereus said.

It is true. I did not order him to do anything. Efrian lifted his head.

"Let's gather the staff in the main ballroom. If it takes me all night, we will find out how the guard was able to escape with Mabyn and where he took her."

***

Efrian stood straight and tall with his hands cupped behind his back as the Erlking walked the ballroom. Darkness poured through the small windows as the many moons of Faery Lands started their descent. What was left of the castle staff was suffering to stand as erect as the Head Guardsman.

The kitchen staff were gathered at the North end of the ballroom. Butlers and chambermaids, serving and cleaning staff, on the East wall, stable hands and groundsmen on the West wall, and everyone else on the South wall. Many were kneeling, hands behind their backs bound with magicked rope. Others lied in the colored pool of their own blood, their wings hacked from their backs, throats slit, or beheaded. Nereus had summoned only fifty guardsmen. They were scattered about the room, all at attention and ready for the Erlking's next order of mutation and/or death.

The Erlking's face blazed in the aftermath of each assault, and Nereus rubbed the mask and often screamed with his own pain. He showed no weakness and exhaustion the likes of which hung over Efrian and the other guardsmen. In fact, just the opposite. The pain seemed to motivate him, excite him, give him strength.

No one had claimed to know who or how the Queen was released, or where she was at this time. It was clear a massive search of the castle and surrounding towns were needed. Efrian silently prayed for the castle search to be first, knowing the more time they stayed inside the further the others were from the castle. The room smelled of death and the sweat of fear.

As the hours went by, Efrian thought of the townsfolk. He knew he could count on no one but himself to let them know of the events of the night. He needed a short reprieve to accomplish this. If Ova and the guard took his wife and child quickly and quietly to the Bad Lands as he directed, the rest of the town needed safety as well. It was not something he'd thought about as he orchestrated this plan earlier with Ova. With a stab of fear, Efrian wondered how he was going explain his family's disappearance, never mind how he was going to evacuate the others before the Erlking's impending meltdown. By the time Nereus reached the townsfolk, he was sure to move from sadistic interrogator and assassin to a manic executor—no questions asked.

"Efrian!" Nereus shouted. "Did you not hear me?"

The Head Guardsman jumped to attention. "No, Sir. I was in thought of a castle search, getting the guards together for their cross-examinations, and any debriefings necessary for attending to the questioning of townsfolks."

The Erlking stared blindly at Efrian for several minutes. That created an eerie silence in the room as everyone still breathing watched and waited.

When Nereus finally spoke, he seemed calm, content, and almost normal. "Go to the guards' quarters, wake Famri, and brief him." His words were as if the two of them were the only ones in the room. "Tell him by sunup I want all guards lined up in front of the death poles. When I am finished here, I will have these guards take the dead there. Also have him order another two rows of poles cut and planted. We will need more, but that is good enough for today.

Nereus let out a short, but very inappropriate, giggle. "Maybe seeing a mound of death waiting for a pole will end all thoughts of rebellion against my crown," his giggle turned into laughter as he tried to push the last words out his mouth, "now... and in... the future."

"Yes, we can hope, my Erlking," Efrian said. "I will go wake Famri, my lord." He started across the large room to leave. "All will be ready for you."

Famri was Nereus's second in command under Efrian, a fire fae, strong in battle, and trustworthy to the throne. So much so, it concerned Efrian. He felt uncomfortable telling the fire fae anything, especially regarding where his own dedication was leading him. *No. I will not openly suggest this never-ending revolt needs to be popped like a puss filled boil to heal. Faery Lands is ready for a new ruler.*

Nereus had become worthy of a painful death. "Wait!" he shouted, and woke Efrian from his thoughts.

Efrian tried to slow the hammering of his heart before taking his hand off the doorknob. "Yes, my Erlking?" he asked, head bowed.

"After you get Famri set, go into town," Nereus said.

Could it get any better than this? Erlking turned his eyes on Nereus. "Yes, my Erlking?"

"Warn the guardsmen's families, then take your wife, son, and the rest of the families to the hive. Order the wasps to watch your family and the others until we settle this. Be sure to check Mabyn is not at the hive. If so, chop off her head and have it sent to me."

"As you order, Sir." Efrian felt giddy. Unsteady. He tightened his grip on the doorknob.

Nereus took in the room around him. "I strongly feel none of my guards would help the queen escape. I bet whoever did this killed Mabyn's guard. I must trust someone, and my guards come first."

The men in uniforms in the ballroom cheered. Nereus turned a smile on them. "My guards, and their families, will be our new nation! A clean and supreme realm!" The Erlking pointed at Efrian. "Your son will lead the next generation of guards, my friend. Now go see that the entitled are safe."

Efrian said, "So it shall be."

Son of a demented jinn, what have I unleashed?

***

As Efrian burst into the guards' quarters, he searched for Famri. The fire fae was leaning against a large stone fireplace and held a cup that sent a thin coil of steam toward the fae's flared nostrils. Efrian strutted toward him.

"Famri, I need you to dispatch fifteen guards to the town square. Have them wait there for further orders from Nereus. Instruct the wood fae to cut and plant two new rows of death poles, immediately. This must be done before sunup. Take the rest the Erlking's guards and line them up in front of the dark garden by sunrise where Nereus will join them."

Although Famri stood at attention, Efrian could sense concern in the ridged nature of the fae's face and body. Efrian took a breath. His own fear was evidently as clear. "There will be interrogations. The queen has disappeared and so far all we know is that her guard is missing as well."

Famri reached for a bottle of brew. He pulled the cork off with his teeth and poured some into the cup he held. He pushed it toward Efrian.

The Head Guardsman waved a hand and shook his head. "No need for that, Famri. Hear this; our Erlking does not believe any of his guardsmen guilty of this horrendous act, including the Queen's guard."

Famri set the bottle on the hearth and recorked it. "That's a relief. I wake every morning and wonder when the guards and their families are next for the poles."

Efrian nodded an agreement. The room would soon begin to rumble with guards arriving for an early meal. Efrian wanted to finish the orders before their arrival. "The townsfolk are next on his interrogation list. He has already talked with the castle staff. Many are ready for the field of death. Let the men know of the queen's disappearance and that the Erlking suspects her guard was killed or captured as well. Encourage conversation and talk among them of the week's events. I'm sure the Erlking will be asking if they saw or heard anything that could lead them to believe there was talk of such a thing among the townsfolk concerning Queen Mabyn. After the remaining guards are questioned, Nereus will move to the town to continue interrogations. He wants the Guardsmen's families to be moved to Reka's hive for their safety. Assure the guards that their wives and children will be well secured by the wasp guards."

"I'm on it, Efrian!" Famri said. "I'll have them up, dressed, and ready directly. They will be told to pack nourishment and fluids." He shook his head. "It looks to be a long day that may go into night, and another day. I'll not have any of our men weakening in the line of duty."

Efrian smiled at his subordinate. "I trust you can handle all here, including morale, until I return?"

"Always." Famri dipped his head and smiled back at Efrian. "And should I return, when they are settled in?"

"Yes," Efrian said, and immediately wished to pull it back. Famri has been vying for the Erlking's attention. Although Efrian did not dislike the fae or have loyalty concerns there was an uncomfortable feeling that Famri somewhat enjoyed the Erlking's torture techniques.

***

When Efrian left, he headed straight for his hut on the outskirts of town. He found it empty as was expected. After a swift check, he realized very little was packed, as should be if they were in flight to the Bad Lands as instructed. A large part of the stress he carried on his shoulders lessened as he left the home he had lived in since becoming a part of the Erlking's guard.

With sadness in his eyes, he stepped out the door and onto the small terrace that faced the street in front of the hut. Bending at the waist, he picked up two, uncooked, green peas, hiding behind the foot of a chair and laid them on the porch table. They rolled left, off the table, and stopped against an unlevel piece of wood near the end of the terrace. A smile spread across his lips and the sadness his eyes held squeezed at his heart. Without looking back, Efrian took flight and headed for the only lights in the villages surrounding the castle. He knew where he was headed, but he did not expect to find what he did when he got to the pavilion.

As Efrian entered the dome, he gasped to see Saul, Ova's lover, on a small stage surrounded by his fellow guardsmen's families. He frantically jutted around the top of the dome searching for his wife among the crowd while Saul's deep baritone voice reverberated off the walls.

"We cannot let him do this to us. The queen is safe. But the rest of us are at the mercy of the Erlking and his morbidity. Who here wants to be hanging on a pole in the death garden? Who here wants to see their husband or children on the poles of death? How many of you have witnessed the suffrage and sadistic deaths of friends and loved ones?"

Fists pumped and voices rose across the pavilion.

"You must warn your husbands! Tell your neighbors! It is time to revolt! Nereus will soon find his queen gone if he hasn't already. He had tortured her enough. If she remained much longer, she would have surely met her death, another head in the Erlking's dark garden."

Efrian spread his wings and flew over the fae below. The crowd ducked and scattered with fear and uncertainty. There was no sign of his family. Efrian ignored his fellow guardsmen's wives and children. He hovered over Saul. "Why are you still here?" he shouted at the castle guard on stage. "And what have you done with my wife and son?!"

CHAPTER FOURTEEN

The Mending

Cal wandered through the forest, his feet shuffling through dry leaves. Behind him the excitement from the fae camp roared as they excitedly tested out their new abilities. Fire, ice, and various other spells shot into the air like fireworks. There were still several half fae left to work with, but Cal was exhausted from all the healing spells he'd had to cast. In all the commotion, he slipped out to find someplace to relax before someone else could find him.

A withered mushroom stood on the forest floor, defiant of the drought. Its cap was wrinkled and turned a rotted brown color, but it still provided enough shade from the days harsh sunlight for Cal to hide under. He slumped down at its base; his head sunk slightly into the soft mushroom stem. It radiated a damp musty smell, but at least it was cool and comfortable.

The birds of the forest squawked and fluttered between the trees, upset by the commotion in the fae camp. Cal kept an eye above as he rested, in case one of the larger birds decided he looked like a midafternoon snack. A black crow darted between branches above, cawing loudly to anything that would listen. A canoe sized feather fluttered from its wing in the commotion and tumbled in the breeze. Cal watched as it danced toward the ground before finally resting at his feet. Its black hairs glistened in the sun. Cal picked it up and twirled it in his hands. Even though it was two times his size, it was still remarkably light. Maybe he would bring it back to the camp with him. He was sure the fae would have a use for it.

Then, out of the corner of his eye, he saw movement. At first, he thought it was nothing more than dust kicked up by an errant gust of wind, but as he turned he saw swirling smoke in a humanoid form approaching. Its bright eyes peering out from the haze sparked memories from deep within Cal. Fear overtook him and before he could think about what he was doing, he had jumped to his feet and materialized his sword in his hand. In a move motivated by pure adrenaline, he brought his blade to rest directly in front of the apparition.

The green and gold smoke drifted backward and offered his hands palm open to the sides. "Apologies," the jinn said calmly. "I should have announced myself; didn't mean to sneak up on you. My name is Aldul. I'm an ally of Coralina and the rebellion."

Cal's senses returned to him, and he relaxed his blade. "Oh, right. Sorry about jumping ya, there," Cal said, vanishing his sword in a burst of light. "Guess I'm a bit on edge."

Aldul relaxed his arms. "Quite alright. I'm familiar with you and your... conflict with Talock. I can't blame you for being more on guard when the jinn are involved."

Cal frowned. "Of course you can. There is only one person I blame for what went down between us, and that's Talock. I don't blame all jinn for that. No one should." With the wave of adrenaline receding, Cal slumped back down against the mushroom. "I just... reacted when I saw you. But I promise, I don't hold any ill will toward you and your people."

Aldul folded his hands in front of his stomach. "That's refreshing to hear. Wish more people felt that way."

"I bet you do." Cal smirked. "Heard this has been a PR nightmare for you guys."

"Amongst a great deal of other incidences," Aldul said. "We're well aware of how the other races view us, as oppressors holding our boots on fae necks. We've certainly received a great deal of pressure from the angels ever since the war. And the younger jinn such as I tend to agree with those sentiments. It's all ancient history for us, one we're more than willing to move on from."

Cal looked up at him. "Does that mean you're here with good news?"

"Indeed. I was on my way to discuss this with Coralina when I saw you resting here," Aldul said, his voice deepened. "It's taken much discussion, and more than a few intense arguments that included everything but physical confrontation. However, in the end, I feel a reasonable conclusion was reached." He floated closer. "We've agreed to send limited support to the rebellion. They decided a full incursion would send the wrong message, as well as weaken Coralina's legitimacy to the crown."

Cal nodded. "I suppose that makes sense. Can't risk the other races fearing Coralina is the same puppet to the jinn as Nereus is. But what exactly does limited support mean?"

"Basically it would entail a small but talented team of jinn to aid in the assault upon the capital. They will be at Coralina's service to be used at her discretion."

Cal scratched his chin. "Oh, kind of like a strike force."

Aldul's glowing eyes focused on him. Even behind the smoky haze, Cal could see the confusion on his face.

"It's a human military term," Cal explained. "Basically, it's a small group of specialists sent for a surgical strike instead of an all-out assault."

Aldul thought about it. "That seems like an accurate description. Jinn are great at infiltration. If the rebels can create enough of a distraction, we'll be able to sneak behind the Erlking's forces and destroy them from within."

Cal smiled. "Well, I think they can manage that." He pointed his thumb back toward the camp. "They just got a powerup and they're just itching to use them."

Aldul turned his attention to the spells soaring above the treetops. "A powerup? You mean the half fae have finally unlocked their abilities? I know Coralina was working with them when I last saw her."

Cal sank his head into the soft mushroom stem. "That's right! Coralina was clever and found a way to use my healing powers to give them a bit of a jump start. It's kind of complicated, but the important thing is it works! That's why I'm out here. Everyone rushed me, wanting to see what new abilities they can unlock. Needed to get out of there for a while and rest before they suck me dry. You'd come back to a bunch of powerful half fae and my husk of a body lying on the ground in the middle of them." Cal snickered. "That was sarcasm by the way," he added.

In Cal's surprise, Aldul laughed. "Yes, I am familiar with the concept," he said. "Believe it or not, jinn do have a sense of humor, dry as it may be." Aldul watched as a tornado of lightning and rock swirled above the camp, dissipating just in time to not do any damage. "I do hope they try to be careful with their newfound abilities, though. We don't need them destroying the resistance before we even reach the capital."

"It's a risk, not going to lie." Cal said. "One of them found out she had gravity defying powers. Half the camp lifted into the air before she even realized what she was doing."

Aldul grew quiet as his eyes bounced between Cal and the camp, his wispy shoulders relaxed. "So, they have grown powerful. We may just have a chance yet."

Cal raised an eyebrow. "You doubted? I mean, you helped to drag the jinn into this situation. You must have thought it was a fight that was winnable."

Aldul shrugged. "A fight worth trying at least. In honesty, I didn't know the likelihood of victory, but Nereus has been a black cloud hovering over the jinn ever since the war, and Coralina and her followers have finally provided us an opportunity to clear it away.

Hopefully for the better." Aldul hesitated and wrung his wrists. "As a fellow outsider to these lands, I feel I can be honest with you, Calastair. I have a doubt as to how much change will come upon these lands in the event of the rebel's victory." His eyes tilted upward to the treetops. "Coralina preaches kind words and seems to believe them. However, I can't shake the feeling that all could change if she is crowned queen. One constant across the realms is the ability of control to corrupt even the most uncorruptible. And while it might be unfair to say, the fae seem particularly susceptible to its power. I fear these lands may be locked in this cycle of revolution for as long as these lands exist."

The honesty took Cal aback. He hadn't expected to find himself in such a conversation today, and certainly not with a jinn. But it was a fair concern, and one that he shared. Coralina was a good friend, one that Cal trusted with his life. However, Aldul was right. Control over others had a way of changing people to their core. Even angels weren't exempt from its corrupting grasp. But of all the fae Cal had met, Coralina had been the most honest with her intentions, and had even warned him before of the fae's selfish nature. He chose to believe she could be the change the faery world needed. Because if not her, then who?

"I wish I could tell you for sure everything will work out with Coralina in power," Cal said. "But I'm not sure I could make that promise for anyone. I mean... how could I? But I feel if anyone here has a chance, it's her. And I'm not willing to just give up on hoping for a better future for the faeries just yet."

Aldul paused and considered what he said. "Alright, fair enough I suppose. I just would hate for the jinn to be behind yet another threat to these lands."

Cal tucked his knees to his chest and wrapped his arms around his legs. "Well, let me put it another way. What do you think will happen if the rebels lose this war?"

The jinn's eyes narrowed. "Nereus would continue his rule over the kingdom, probably tighten his grip over the people as well."

"More than that," Cal said. "He'd bring the doom of this land. Nereus isn't the kind of person who lets bygones be bygones. The jinn, the angels, we've both taken a stand, and have sided with his enemies. He won't let that go. As soon as he's done with the rebels he'll turn his soldiers against us."

Aldul shook his head. "I can't believe he'd be that reckless. His army would be in no condition to wage another war on that scale, not for a long time. And if he dared to attack the jinn in a weakened state—"

"He will," Cal interrupted. "To him, allowing someone to go against him unpunished would be the same as defeat. And once he attacks the jinn, they'll invade full force, leaving this land in ruin this time. And even if he didn't pick a fight with your people, eventually his iron fist would slowly choke the life out of the fae until they fade away. There is no future for the faeries till Nereus is removed."

Aldul crossed his arms. "So, gamble on Coralina or leave the land to certain destruction. I suppose that's not much of a choice."

"I'll take a chance, even if it's a slim one, over certain ruin any day."

Aldul sighed. "Well, in a strange way, that does make me feel better. I'm just desperate to avoid making the same mistakes those before me made."

Cal laughed. "I suppose that's the trick, isn't it? I'm afraid I can't help much with that; seems like half my life is making mistakes and trying to glue everything back together afterward."

Aldul opened his arms. "Well, I appreciate you spending the time to talk with me."

"Sure, no problem," Cal said, crossing his arms behind his neck. "Now if you don't mind, I'd like to get a bit of rest before getting back to helping the other half fae."

Aldul hesitated. "Actually, there's another reason I wanted to meet with you. And I promise it won't take long."

Cal closed his eyes. "Alright, but just know I don't know how much help I'll be. Think I used the rest of my energy on our last discussion."

"Actually, this time I want to help you," Cal heard from behind his eyelids. "See, there's more crimes committed by Talock that needed to be rectified. He's made enemies everywhere he went, manipulating everything in his path. You were unlucky enough to get caught up in his path and paid for it."

Cal opened his eyes and focused on the jinn. "That's a way to put it, I guess. But why would you and the rest of the jinn council care about it, in the middle of everything going on?"

"One of our own maiming an angel? That's not exactly a small event now is it? The relationship between the jinn and heaven has always been tense, and your father has been breathing down our necks ever since the attack on you."

Cal scoffed and waved his hand. "Look, I don't need any restitutions or... I don't know, gift baskets from you. I'm comfortable leaving what happened in the past and just trying to move on."

Aldul floated closer. "I'm willing to offer you more than... gift baskets. I'm here to offer you a chance to fix your wing."

Cal stared at the jinn. He was uncertain how to react. There was an appreciation for what Aldul was trying to do within him, but an anger brewed as well as he scratched open an old wound. "There is no fixing my wing. I was forced to destroy what was left of it to stop Talock and his hideous plan. Once destroyed, angel wings can never be remade. That's even above our abilities."

Aldul bowed his head. "Yes, and above ours as well. I suppose I misspoke. What I offer isn't so much a fix, but a prosthetic. One that might not be as good as what you had but would give you basic function of a wing."

Cal narrowed his eyes. "And how exactly would you be able to do that?" he asked skeptically.

The smoke wisps around Aldul's mouth curled into a smile. "Here, I'll show you. Stand up."

Cal hesitated.

"What I plan to do can be easily undone if you wish. There's no need to worry."

Cal slowly stood; his right wing draped over his shoulder. He was unsure if he liked the hopeful feeling bubbling in his chest. "Okay, what now?" he asked.

"Just relax." Aldul clasped his hands in front of himself. Green and gold smoke seeped through his fingers and drifted toward the ground. The mound of smoke slithered toward Cal, swirling and winding over itself. For a moment, Cal thought this could be a trap, some devious ploy to get him to let his guard down. But he pushed that reaction down, reminding himself this wasn't Talock, and that Aldul wasn't the enemy.

The tendrils of smoke climbed up his left leg and seeped up his side. He lost sight of it around the shoulder, and if it was doing anything he couldn't feel it. Eventually, Aldul lowered his hands, and the trail of smoke disappeared. Cal frowned. "Didn't work, did it?" He tried to sound indifferent, but disappointment leaked through his voice.

Aldul smiled. "It worked perfectly, Try to bend your left wing."

Cal was confused. He felt nothing there, but tried to flex it anyway. As he did, a wing made of green smoke and shimmering gold light draped over his left shoulder.

"It's going to feel strange at first," Aldul said. "It has no weight to it like your other one. But it's fully functional. Give it a try."

Cal hardly heard his words. He was transfixed with the shimmering gold light pulsing through his new wing, wondering if it could really work. With a sudden burst of curiosity, he flapped both wings hard, and to his surprise, he lifted into the air. Aldul was right, it did feel different. He found it hard at first to balance himself with the different weight of the wings. But after a few minutes, he began to get a feel for the different forces he needed to apply.

He shot upward, past the squawking crow and above the tree branches. As he breached the top, the faery world opened up before him. He could see the silver hills off in the distance, and the Erlking's castle off to the south. It was a sensation he hadn't felt in quite a while. It was the feeling of true freedom.

Cal floated downward and landed in front of Aldul. "Thank you," he said with a wide smile, a salty tear running past his lips. "I mean... this is... just the best."

Aldul bowed his head. "It's the least I could do to help a new friend. Now, should we brief Coralina?"

Cal laughed. "No. I'll leave that honor to you. I got some flying to do."

CHAPTER FIFTEEN

The Beginning of the End

"I'm pleased you did not alert the other villages, Saul," Efrian said. "It would have meant your life by order of the Erlking and most likely by my hand."

"I'm not ignorant, Sir," Saul replied. "But I cannot stand by while innocent—"

"That's enough, Saul," Efrian said. "I understand, and that is why I am here. Where are my wife and son?"

Below the stage, murmurs trembled through the crowd.

Saul stiffly stood next to Efrian on the platform in the Pavilion. He unnecessarily cleared his throat, and, in a very soft voice, replied, "Ova and your family are safe... as you instructed."

"Thank you," Efrian said. "And although I appreciate your need to inform the guards' families of your concerns, I don't believe gearing them for a conflict is needed at the moment. The Erlking has declared guards are not responsible. He thought you dead by the hands of his enemies and praised your dedication. I think we need to keep it that way."

Efrian turned to the wives and children of his fellow guards. "Nereus instructed I have all of you taken to the hive and secure your safety with the wasp guards while he questions the villagers around the castle about the event that occurred this evening. He is of the mind that after he finds the culprits and gets rid of the last of the half breeds, all of you will prosper. He looks forward to your procreation of a more perfect fae realm for our future generations. So, for the moment, you are his dream come true. You must be protected."

Efrian could see Saul's temperament ease somewhat but his cause was clear in the deepening color of his blue eyes. He held Efrian's gaze over thin lips and a jaw tight enough to color his cheeks. Efrian patted Saul on the shoulder and his voice filled the stadium. "If I had known Nereus was going to take this turn, I would not have contacted my family. At the time, I felt their heads would be the first hanging on a death pole in the dark garden next to mine."

With heaviness of body and sorrow squeezing his heart, Efrian scanned the room filled with faeries he and his wife knew well. His eyes stopped on the children they had taken into their home and the ones who returned the favor while parents visited outlying villages before the much-needed curse fell upon Nereus. Those outlying villages no longer existed. "Jynifer and Jaris would have been safer at the hive with all of you. Instead, in my haste, I sent them away this morning."

"Do you want me to find them and bring them to the hive?" Saul asked as an aside.

A whispering of hope hung in the air.

"No," Efrian whispered. "But I do want you to find Coralina, Rampart, and Mabyn. Tell them of all the activities here, and where the families are located in case we need to relocate them."

"But—"

"No buts, Saul. Famri will be here soon with guards. I asked him to move everyone to the hive, as Nereus ordered." Efrian forced a grin. "Remember, you are supposed to be dead. But today, you have made me proud, my friend."

"Thank you, Sir." Saul's blue eyes lightened with the shared knowledge of the queen's disappearance. "And what are your intentions?"

"Other than to get Famri moving toward the hive," Efrian whispered, "I need others to feel as you and I do about our situation with the Erlking."

Saul smiled. "A good number of guardsmen, and even of the ones that are not," his eyes scanned the room, "their families certainly are. I'm comfortable talking to the women."

Efrian reached out and captured Saul's hand, pulling him close to his chest. He patted Saul's back as hope was replaced with comradery-driven courage. "Good," he whispered in the guard's ear. "I need a list of those that are definitively trustworthy before Famri arrives. Your job in the Bad Lands will be to inform the revolutionists it is time, and we are making ready to receive them in Copper Groves."

"Why there, Sir?" Saul asked. "It was the first to be destroyed by the Erlking's madness."

Efrian smiled. "Yes, but woods surrounding Copper Groves will give a large group the ability to get close to the castle before being seen, and it's the town closest to the hive."

"You should come with us, Sir. Today." Saul's knitted brows and slightly turned down lips made Efrian smile.

"Someone needs to inform our comrades," Efrian said. "Have Coralina and Rampart make ready. It won't be long. On that list, pick one exceptionally trustworthy guardsmen, and I will see he or she accompanies me into town with Nereus. I hope everyone will be safe by end of the day."

Saul started to speak and Efrian put a hand on the water fae's arm. "I will handle my family's disappearance."

"You sure?"

"Yes," Efrian said with a glance at a fae woman in the audience. "With a little help from a friend. Now move. I will see you soon."

"Okay, I'll head to the woods on the East side of town. After dispatching Famri, meet me there. I'll have the information you requested."

***

"How did you get them gathered so quickly?" Famri asked Efrian as his eyes swept the dome with suspicion.

Before Efrian could speak, a water fae close to the stage flew forward. "My family helped," she said.

Maribelle had sea-blue eyes and skin the color of moss on rocks near the edge of a slow-moving stream. Soft waves of foamy white hair rippled over her shoulders. The underling gripping her hand smiled up at him. Efrian knew the woman and her son well.

"I'm an early riser, Famri," Maribelle said. "I had seen Efrian fly into town very early this morning." Maribelle paused to glance at Efrian. "He and his wife live nearby. I was outside when Jynifer came over to tell me you were coming to gather us. Although she offered no reason, and without further question, I took it upon myself to help." Maribelle bowed her head. "I hope I did not overstep my bounds."

Efrian and Famri smiled at the water fae and she continued. "I immediately woke my boys and told them to wake only the other guards' families and direct them here. Is our Erlking all right?"

"Yes, he is fine," Efrian said with a knowing look at his neighbor. "And Famri and I thank you for that, Maribelle." Efrian hoped the next question would fly as smoothly. "And did my wife gather the first group and head to ready the hive?"

"Yes, as your wife was told," Maribelle said, "she left right after telling me."

"And you are sure none of the villagers have been made aware?" Famri crustily asked without a word as to why Efrian had sent his wife on a trip without protection.

"I am sure," Maribelle said. "I had asked the wind fae to apply a blanket of sleep over the rest of the town huts as all the families arrived here. It will be several hours before they wake. We moved swiftly and quietly to the dome, although that did not stop the questions once we arrived. I'm sure everyone will be pleased to find the Erlking is well."

Famri's jaw tightened. "Well, not altogether, I'm afraid. Queen Mabyn is still missing. That is the reason for this evacuation and your safety."

***

Famri was being bombarded with questions about the queen to the point he felt he was being sidetracked. He had to remind himself he was the one that told them.

When they finally left the village, he guided them around the Northeastern side of the castle and circled left toward the hive. The woods were rich with green leaves and brown trunks. He had men posted around the outside of the group as if herding them to their destination. When a small grassy field appeared ahead of them, Famri darted above them, a short reprieve from the constant chatter. The crowd of fae looked like a lost swarm of bees searching for a new home. The thought made him laugh. It was times like this that made Famri smile. He had no desire to find a mate. He hated children and did not need a bossy wife. Famri told himself he would never allow the Erlking to force him into breeding a family. That would take too much of his time... He had dedicated his life to his job, and someday hoped to be in Efrian's boots.

The silence of the harpy women's chatter below was replaced with the soft whirr of his wings, and that was comforting. He took a moment to closely observe the surroundings. It had been a long time since he delved further than the castle grounds and the Woodline at the fringe of the new villages.

At first, Famri did not notice the trees were darker and the grassy field was dry and lifeless, as if there had been no rain for months. Ahead of him, a small brown incaved area looked to be a dried-out pond. This left an uncomfortable feeling in the pit of his stomach that he could not identify. He was so absorbed in this feeling that the forest came upon him swifter than anticipated.

Famri dove downward and followed the grouping of fae into the trees. The woods seemed darker than usual, but not enough to cause concern.

The faeries were on foot now. Walking slowly, wings tight against their backs. The bottom of the trees were black, and dark roots reached out of the ground as if searching for something. A streambed was nearby, but there was no sound of moving water. Famri flew nearer to the stream and was joined by one of his guards.

"It's bone dry, Famri," the guard said.

"I can see that."

"Did you notice the grass in the field was dry, Sir?" the guard said. "With the amount of rain we've had in the last of four weeks, it is highly unlikely the grass could be in such a state." He stared at Famri with a wrinkled forehead and tight lips. "Do you think we should warn the Erlking that someone may have cast a spell on our kingdom?"

Famri turned to find a mumbling group of fae women coming their way. "All right! Enough rest. Let's move on! There is nothing of concern here."

The faeries obeyed but their steps were slower. Their widespread muttering of discord was of no concern at the moment.

As the group moved further into the woods, the trees became darker and darker as a blackness climbed the trunks. Soon, the leaves were gone and the branches were black skeletal arms against a sunlit sky.

Another lifeless field peeked through the trees and soon displayed an even more barren forest on the other side. The hive was several yards into those trees. The group gathered at the edge of the field. Their silence gave strength to the sound of dead grass crunching under foot as they began to walk again, heads lowered, eyes watching their feet. They continued this way along a dusty path, lined with charcoal-colored trees, that led to the hive.

Yards into the dark and foreboding forest one of the guards shouted, "Famri, what is that?"

The startled faeries froze, all eyes on the trunk of a large black tree, near the hive, a few yards away.

"Do not move!" came a loud voice in the distance, followed by an increasingly loud buzzing noise.

A swarm of wasps exploded from the nest and headed for them.

"What is your business here?" one of the wasps asked.

"The Erlking has ordered his guards' families be given refuge here," Famri barked. "Queen Mabyn is missing."

The wasps circled; their buzzing became louder. Some of the faeries covered their ears with their hands or wings.

"We will guide you slowly toward the hive while giving the portals of that tree a large berth," said the wasp that seemed to be a leader. "Understand?"

"We will help keep them in a tight group," Famri answered. He turned to the faeries. "Let's move slowly and quietly."

As they moved past the two large wavering holes in the air behind and below the crumpling black tree, they saw gray clouds floating on an Earthly sky through the upper portal and nothing but blackness in the one below the stump.

A rumbling came from the lower portal.

"Everyone! Move quickly now!" the lead wasp shouted.

"Yes, follow us!" another bellowed and zipped by, herding the group into a tighter circle.

As the circle began to move again, two things happened. A gorgon with black skin and gray eyes came from the lower portal, followed by the horn and then the face of a gigantic cyclops. Second, a frenzy of frightened buzzing preceded a tightening of their grouping and the fae picked up speed as they headed in the direction the wasps were guiding them.

The cyclops reacted quickly and took only four swift steps before it was upon them. The ugly creature raised a fat-fingered hand, snatched the feet of an older fae, and popped her into its mouth. The large eye in the middle of its forehead closed as he chewed. The gorgon's manic laughter filled the air while long fingernails clicked as her arm reached toward them. The white snakes on her head hissed and struck out at the fae above her head and barely missed their mark.

Famri and his men pulled bows, and soon after arrows filled the air. As the ground trembled with the cyclops's steps the guardsmen lured the creature into the fae sunlight. It stumbled and stepped back into the barren woods, then turned and headed in the other direction. The gorgon's laughter faded to an echo.

The remaining families clamored and tightened their circle to protect the children within. Many were already in the hive and the rest slid in quickly with the Erlking's wasps pushing them inside.

Famri and the last of the guards followed the cyclops but kept their distance. As they got closer to the portals, they saw no one and paused to look inside. Snow fell on trees from behind the open, upper portal. And sparks from a fire deep within the second portal floated up and above their heads.

"Damn, what the hell is this?" a guard asked. "Can we seal them off?"

"I don't know," Famri spat with fear in his eyes. "I'm going to head back to the castle for help. The rest of you stay with the families inside of the hive. Talk to the wasp leader to see what he knows. I have a feeling our kingdom is dying and the bottom portal is spewing entrails from hell to feed on the living." His eyes moved from the portals to his men. "The Bad Lands are expanding."

CHAPTER SIXTEEN

Battle Plans

Famri's wings burned as the castle came into view. In his rush to report to the Erlking, he pushed himself forward from the hive directly to the castle. A strong breeze at his back let him glide, giving his muscles the first much-needed break. The capital city stretched beneath him. Fae roamed the streets, but even at his height, Famri could sense a hesitation in their movement as though a dark cloud hung over the city. It was a feeling Famri was familiar with, the dark thoughts of approaching war. Every day it grew in the minds of the people. Everyone knew ... no ... wished the conflict would come to an end. And the longer it took, the deeper the fears of living under Nereus's rule burrowed. It wasn't his Erlking's fault. All Nereus wanted was a true and clean brood of fae as it should be.

Famri glided toward the castle's large wooden entry, and slowly descended with fluttering wings. The two guardsmen posted on either side tensed and then tilted their spears toward each other to block entrance. As their second in command got closer, the guardsmen unlocked spears, grabbed the door handles, and pulled them open for him. Famri landed but didn't slow, his bare feet slapping against cold stone as he rushed through the castle door and down the main hallway.

There was more traffic throughout the castle than normal, mostly soldiers moving in groups. The added security made the large halls feel suffocatingly small. Famri tucked his wings close and pushed through the lines and into an empty throne room. "Hey!" he shouted to one of the four guards standing near to the red cushioned chair spackled with jewels and green painted leaves over its tall wooden back. "Where is the Erlking? I must report to him immediately."

A thin female fae standing near a more threadlike male said, "The king is in the Southeast conference room with advisers. While he didn't ask for privacy, I'm not sure he would be receptive to interruptions."

Famri swallowed. This was one of the hardest parts of being in the king's court, walking the tightrope of what would anger the Erlking more, incurring his wrath by interruption, or by not immediately reporting important information. And sometimes the answer to that was solely dependent on the king's mood of the day. Picking wrong could have... serious consequences.

In the end, Famri would rather risk the anger by reporting, than look weak and hesitant, two traits the Erlking detested among his guard leaders. Bowing his head, Famri headed up the winding stairs to the conference room. Every step grew heavier as he neared the room and doubted his decision. Two guards Famri knew well adorned the door, their ceremonial spears crossed.

"Clear the way," Famri commanded. "I need passage to the Erlking, straightaway."

They fae complied but exchanged concerned glances.

Famri leaned forward and whispered, "How is the Erlking's mood today?"

The left one leaned close to Famri's ear. "He seemed in a decent mood when they entered," he whispered back. "But we've heard him raise his voice many a time since. I cannot guarantee how charitable he's feeling at the moment."

Famri grunted and, taking a deep breath, pushed through the heavy doors. Once inside, he saw the Erlking standing at the end of a long table, his two advisors stood next to him with their arms clasped respectfully in front of them. They were twins, brother and sister, who had been a part of the Erlking's court since their father took council with the king. Their long white hair trailed delicately over silver garbed shoulders, and two sets of weary eyes fell on him.

Famri dropped to his knee and bowed his head. "Apologies for the interruption, my lord," he said, trying to keep his voice from quaking. "I have a report from my post I thought you'd want to hear on my return from the hive."

The Erlking rapped his fingers on a chair he stood behind. "And you thought it more important than what I could be discussing with my two chief advisors?" he asked with a smooth and silky voice.

Famri closed his eyes as he tried to think of a diplomatic answer. "I fear it may be," he said, immediately regretting using the word fear.

From the other side of the table, Famri could hear the Erlking draw a long deep breath. "Very well," he said, turning to his advisors. "If you would excuse us."

The twins walked calmly out of the room and looked upon Famri with amusement. As soon as the heavy doors closed, the Erlking stepped closer to his guardsman. "Rise, my friend," he said, gesturing with his palms open toward the ceiling. "What have you come to report?"

Famri stood, taking special care not to hold the Erlking's gaze too long as to look disrespectful, but not too short to risk looking sheepish. "My lord, I was out patrolling the northeastern lands of the castle. The further out I patrolled the more distressed I found the lands. Fields and forest alike seemed to be dying without reason. And worse yet, the decay seems to be attracting the attention of demonic beings. I bared witness to a gorgon and cyclops emerging from the portal outside of the hive, and I fear others could be gathering at other gates."

If the Erlking was concerned by the news, he didn't show it. His expression remained cold as he slowly nodded. "Interesting," was all he said as he slid the chair at the head of the table back and sat in it. He clasped his hands together on the table and seemed lost in thought.

"I fear," Famri continued, "if we are unable to find the reason for the death of the forest, it may affect the lands closer to the capital. Moreover, we could become overrun by otherworldly creatures."

The Erlking tapped either side of his chin with index finger before gesturing to the chair beside him. "Have a seat," he said calmly.

Famri hesitated. Sitting at the table with the king was an honor reserved for those who provided a great service to the throne, and not for those baring bad news. Though confused, he didn't dare not do what he was commanded. Famri slipped into the chair quietly.

The Erlking leaned close enough that Famri could smell the leather from his mask. "Now, what I'm about to tell you doesn't leave this room under penalty of death," the Erlking said. "Do you understand?"

Famri nodded and tried to tuck spit under his tongue so as not to swallow hard.

"The faery lands aren't being dried by some curse or evil beings; it is I who has drained the water from the forest," the Erlking said matter-of-factly. "It was a way to force the rebellion into making their final effort against me, leaving no land of which they could seek shelter and hide from us. They will need to push forward their assault or risk being picked off as their situation grows dire. For now, I hold the water in the Lake of Life below, supplying the lands nearby so our farms don't suffer. And when the rebellion is destroyed fully, I'll allow the water back into the rest of the forest."

Famri lost charge of the liquid building around his tongue, swallowed hard, and struggled not to look shocked. Of all the reasons the land could be dying, he never would have guessed the Erlking was responsible. That explained why the Erlking was increasing protection around the castle. He was trying to draw the rebellion close enough to command from inside. As he thought on it, a cruel smile grew. "That is genius, my lord. The land will recover, and the rebels won't be able to hide from our scouts in the underbrush."

"Indeed."

"But what of the creatures and the portals?"

"What of them?" Nereus opened his hands. "All they do is provide another whip for the rebels to march forward. Once the water is restored, the portals will stabilize once again and the remaining demons will be taken care of. Sure, we'll lose some people who are still on the outskirts, but that is the way of war."

The light behind Nereus's mask flickered, causing him to grit his teeth. Famri pretended not to notice. "Of course, your Highness."

The Erlking smiled. "I'm glad you see the wisdom behind this move. Efrian seemed disturbed the night I drained the forest. He would never say so of course, but I do worry he might not have the stomach for this work as I thought he would." Nereus stood and placed a heavy hand on Famri's shoulder. "I know what's in your heart. I've seen the determination flicker in the eyes of many others. Ozil, Efrian, they all had the same drive that led them to be the captain of the guard. But Ozil chose to betray us at what could have been our greatest hour, and my confidence in Efrian weakens. If you do well in the coming days, you could very well find yourself taking his place at my side."

The fear within Famri subsided. The confirmation of the Erlking's approval slaked his need for appreciation. A surge of pride coursed through his chest. "I'll make you proud, my Erlking. What is it you ask of me?"

"Gather six of your most trusted men," Nereus commanded. "It will be your detail's responsibility to stay close to me as my personal guard for the next few days. Never mind what happens on the outskirts, our focus is on the capital. I feel the wives of the guard are safer where you left them than out there." Nereus pointed toward the villages. "When Coralina attacks, and she will, you and your men will oversee my protection in the unlikely chance the rebels breech our walls." Nereus smiled. "Do this, and you will find my favor rewarding."

***

"I hate the smell of this town," Dusk groaned. He walked next to Rampart with an invisibility spell draped over him to avoid attention.

"Too many fae in one area from too many walks of life. It gets, confusing."

Rampart chuckled as he clinched a ragged hood over his face. "Honestly, Dusk, I can't remember the last time we went anywhere you didn't find something to complain about. Is there anything that gives you joy?"

"Ahh, yes, walking in the fiery lakes of the underworld, the smell of brimstone floating in the air while the screams of the dammed ring out."

Even though he was invisible, Rampart knew the toothy grin he bore.

"The comforts of home, ay?" Rampart rolled his eyes and tugged at his shirt.

In order to hide his imp wings, he had wrapped them around himself and tucked them into his clothing. The effect looked bulkier than he'd like, but it worked. With a pair of regular faery wings glamoured on his back, no one spared a second look in his direction. He was worried the guardsman might recognize him, but he found dressed in refugee disguise the guards had gone out of their way to avoid him. But just in case, Rampart always had a glamour spell at the ready should someone draw too close.

Rampart peeked down the alleyway they waited in, but only found the cool night air waiting for him. The capital was quiet once the sun went down due to the guard patrols intensifying at night, and the later it got, the less tolerant they became.

"I don't think this guy is coming," Dusk grunted. "He's almost an hour late."

Rampart sighed and slumped against the wall. "Be patient. He probably just got caught up," he said. "It's hard for resistance members to move around at night."

"He's probably dead." Rampart could feel the hell hound's hot breath on his side as the animal spoke. "The longer we stay here, the more at risk we are of meeting the same fate."

Rampart crossed his arms. "We stay until we are sure," he said, quietly but sternly. "It's too important to leave now."

"Heh heh, sure, whatever you say. Just know if push comes to shove, I'm not above leaving you in a human heartbeat."

Rampart let out a chuckle, even though he knew the hellhound wasn't joking. He had made contact when he arrived with people who were part of the capital resistance. It took time and convincing, but they finally set up a meeting with their local leader. But as the night dragged on, it seemed more and more likely Dusk was right and the fae was captured, or even that his contact had lied about the meet just to get rid of them.

As Rampart was ready to call it quits, a shadowy figure turned the corner, covered in a long black cloak. As he approached, Rampart cast a shadow spell over his face, not enough to look suspicious, but enough to hide his features. When the man walked past, Rampart kicked over a nearby bottle.

The figure stopped. "Must be careful, water is in short supply under blue moons."

"Except in the silver hills," Rampart responded in a deep voice. Such codes always seemed silly to him, but effective enough.

"Apologies for my tardiness," the man said without turning toward him. "The patrols have increased and made travel difficult."

"Completely understandable. I'm just glad you were able to meet with us."

The cloaked head nodded. "A friend in common told me you brought word from Coralina and the resistance."

Dusk shifted. "Not so fast," he barked. "How do we know you actually work for the capital resistance?"

Rampart expected the mysterious figure to react to the disembodied voice, but instead he froze in place. "Dusk?" he asked, turning slightly toward them. "Rampart?"

Rampart reached and pulled back the man's hood, reveling Efrian underneath.

Rampart's blood instantly began to boil. In a quick motion, he grabbed Efrian by the collar and pinned him against the side of the building. "What the hell are you doing here, Efrian?!"

Efrian raised his hands to his side. "I'm with the capital resistance."

"Bullshit," Rampart spat. "You're here under the Erlking's orders, sent to infiltrate and turn the rebels into the guard. Looking for another promotion?"

"No, I swear."

"I don't believe you."

Dusk growled. "Enough. I know how to settle this." The hound moved behind Rampart and breathed fire on the ground. It licked the dirt, leaving fiery symbols behind till they formed a circle. "Now, step in it," he commanded Efrian.

"I'm not a fool, Dusk. I don't step into glyphs I don't recognize. Especially ones left by hellhounds."

Dusk laughed. "It's a glyph of truth. If you stand on it and speak nothing but truth, you have nothing to fear. If you stand on it and lie, you'll be turned to ash even before you feel the flame."

Rampart released him. "Either way works for me."

Efrian scowled, but reluctantly stepped into the circle. He put his hands to the side, palm out. "I'm part of the capital resistance and am not sent to infiltrate for the Erlking." He waited a moment, and after nothing happened, he shrugged. "There. Convinced?"

Dusk chuckled. "Great. Now give me a list of your worst fears."

"Dusk!" Rampart snapped.

"Fine, fine. I'll release the seal."

The fiery symbols disappeared, leaving the dirt as it was.

Rampart sighed. "I believe you," he said. "But joining us at the end of the war doesn't wipe away everything you've done since taking my role as Ozil's right hand man."

"I wouldn't ask that of anyone," Efrian said. "However, I would remind you I'm hardly the only one to be sold on the promise of glory for serving the throne and kingdom."

Rampart scoffed. Even though what he said was true, Rampart wasn't capable of giving him the benefit of the doubt. He crossed his arms and leaned against the building.

"So," Efrian said, and straightened his cloak. "Why did Coralina send you to the capital?"

"She wanted me to help organize the rebels within the city. She marches toward the capital for our final attempt to unseat Nereus."

Efrian smiled. "Then we are on the same page. I just sent a messenger to Coralina to inform her we are ready to receive her soldiers."

Rampart glared at him. "Who did you send?"

"Don't worry, it's someone I trust."

"Excuse me if that doesn't make me feel better," Rampart said. "We have to make sure when they get here the resistance is ready to take to the streets and disrupt the guard from within while the half fae attack from the front."

Efrian nodded. "It will need to be handled carefully. The spirit in our ranks is high, but our numbers are few. If we don't tread carefully, the guard will tear through our ranks before Coralina even steps foot within the capital."

"You don't need to charge headfirst into the enemy to disrupt them," Rampart said. "We can barricade streets, force them where we want them to go. Be thorns in their sides and glass in their boots. Anything to slow them, create chaos behind their lines."

Efrian put his hands on his hips. "Agreed, but here is not the place to plan such things. I'll bring you to our camp, and we can work out exactly how we're going to move."

CHAPTER SEVENTEEN

Those that Wander are Often Not Lost

Two guards stood to watch at the entrance to a large room within the hive. Behind the doors, Saul stood on a platform in the center of the room. All the family members were gathered in front of the guard that saved their queen.

"Our lands are dying," Saul said.

"Yes, and how do we survive on honey alone?" a female with short white hair and a bulbous nose asked.

"Let's not rush toward negativity, Mae." Maribelle smiled at the white-haired woman. "I'm sure Reka, the hive's previous resident, has a fair supply of nourishment stored within the hive."

"This is true." One of the wasp guards stepped forward. "It is well-stocked and well-guarded."

"What about water?" asked a mother with a high-pitched voice. She looked down at the two little ones attached to her hands and jerked one of them back into place as he tried to scramble away.

Saul motioned to one of the guards. "Can you send a small swarm to seek water?"

"No need, Sir," the wasp that had spoken previously said. "We make weekly trips through the upper portal that leads to a land called Down Under. There is a small stream and we carry water back to the hive."

"Do you feel this is wise now that our arrival is known?" Saul asked. "The creatures we witnessed came from the portal directly below. They will be more diligent knowing you need more food and water for us."

"True," the guard said. "But the lower portal leads to the Netherworld, Sir. It only took us once to realize we should keep from going in that direction. And the beasts below have never caused us an issue—"

"—until our arrival." Saul fanned the room with his hand. "May I remind you how precious these families are?"

"No, Sir. They are safe inside. There are many cells and cribs for them to hide. The hive itself is indestructible due to the Erlking's magic wards. Nothing from Netherworld, uninvited, can touch its surface without destruction."

"And what about this Down Under place?" a male fae shouted. He looked to be a bit older than most of the children, but still an underling.

"A good question, lad," the guard said. "We found this to be a level under Earth. It seems a friendly realm. Fae have traveled in and out of that portal for hundreds of years. It's a land of passage into the human world. We have never been stopped or questioned when there. I give you my word."

"Why do I need your word if I have your loyalty?" Saul asked.

"It is a well-known saying to ward off concern, Sir. Nothing more." The wasp guard's wings buzzed his frustration.

The other guard stepped forward. "By the order of our Erlking, we will protect the families

to our deaths."

"This is our word." The first guard landed in position by the door. "And with due respect, Sir, anything we suggest comes from years of experience and should not be doubted."

Saul paused, eyes hard, jaw clenched while he considered the consequences should he poke the wasp he knew reported to Nereus daily.

"Alright," Saul said, "it is clear we both have the best interests of the king's precious cargo. So, while they are here, the creatures entering through the portals must be monitored. We will dispatch a swarm to make rounds twice a day, early morning before light dances with shadows and each night after darkness pushes daylight aside.

"Efrian should be informing Nereus of their safe arrival at this moment. I'm sure we will be safely transporting all of you back, soon. For now, they will all stay inside."

Saul, knowing he was one breath away from death, conceded. "I will leave their safety in the proficient care of your hive. I must leave for a few days and continue my search for Queen Mabyn. Granted life by the sun and the moons, I will continue to be worthy of their graces."

***

The voice of Famri, Efrian's second in command, wafted down halls of the castle. "Fae, real fae, will be nothing more than folklore in the future if we continue to accept half breeds are fae."

Efrian took note of his second in command's boisterous bravado as Famri turned a corner and came into view, accompanied by a younger guard. Neither of them noticed Efrian and he continued toward Nereus's chart room.

"This is why our king wants an end to the revolution and the filth their kind has created," Famri said, eyes glued to his subordinate as he slapped the young guardsman on the back. "If you could've seen the lands outside of our towns. They are drying up and dying. But it won't be long before Nereus ends this and all will be—"

"Famri!" Efrian shouted in a jovial tone. "Good to find you educating our undergraduates. It makes me proud."

Efrian's words clearly took his second in command by surprise. The fae stumbled over his own feet, causing the young guardsman to try to assist in keeping Famri from bouncing off the corner of a wall.

The fury of Famri's embarrassment sent off a stream of defamatory words for the underling accompanying him that ended with a shaking head and forced eye contact with Efrian. "Thank you, Sir. If I can only teach them to walk and talk at the same time without tripping their superiors." He flogged the junior guardsman with the back of his hand.

Efrian burst into laughter. "Ah, well, we have both been in his shoes. And if I remember correctly," Efrian's eyes turned hard, "your transgressions were swiftly turned to dedication."

Efrian paused and caused Famri to break their locked eyes.

Chin dipped; head slightly tilted. With eyes wide, Famri glanced up at his superior. "Yes, Sir. I would give my life for you."

"Carry on, Famri," Efrian said, and moved past him with a nod of his head.

The guardsman's wide eyes and slight tilt of head was an expression Efrian knew well. It was Famri's tell. He was lying. This was one of Efrian's gifts. Even as a child, he knew when anyone lied simply by judging their body language as they spoke. *Not anyone,* his inner voice chided. *You have yet to discern Nereus's tell.*

"I will," Efrian mumbled to himself as he turned the corner where Famri had come from and left the two behind. *I wonder what my second in command has been reporting to my Erlking without my order.*

Efrian pulled open the heavy door of the chart room to find Nereus ready to leave for town. The Erlking extended his hand. "You have always had perfect timing, my friend," Nereus said. "I assume you ran into your second in the hall?"

"Indeed," Efrian said, "with one of our trainees. He seemed as surprised as I, since I gave him no orders to report. I hope he was not a bother, Your Highness."

"Not at all," the Erlking replied. "In fact, he was enlightening."

As they walked down the halls and out into the courtyard where guardsmen were lined up and ready for the trip to town, no other words were spoken.

When they were walking in the field toward the villages, close on the horizon, Nereus addressed Efrian. "Why did you order Famri to accomplish a task I felt important enough to order you to perform?"

Efrian was swift to answer after the issue in the hall with Famri. "I felt needed here, Sir. And Famri is weak in making his own decisions during directed tasks. He needs to learn not to simply stay on track but to improvise, when needed, for the betterment of the outcome."

"I feel there is strength in executing a command from a superior, as the superior directed," Nereus said. "No matter the outcome."

Efrian took pause and swallowed hard. The synchronized steps of the guardsmen marching behind them in sync with his heartbeats made it difficult to concentrate. Step-beat-beat. Step-beat-beat. Step-beat-beat. He had not seen this coming. Had the Erlking lost faith in him?

"Yes, my Erlking, that is often true," Efrian said, and paused for a heartbeat. "Unless doing so destroys the wishes of my Erlking and jeopardizes his realm. Often direction needs tweaking to accomplish what is expected when a roadblock appears. The open portal with underworld creatures was unexpected."

"Indeed," Nereus said. "And from what Famri said, was handled flawlessly."

"Agreed," Efrian, "but his decision to come back to ask for help with the underworld creatures was not."

"What do you mean?" Nereus asked.

"Famri should have sent a guardsman and a few wasps for help," Efrian said, "and stayed to protect the precious cargo and our hope for the fruition of a perfect generation."

As they approached, villagers stood in a long straight line with a depth that was immeasurable from their location. Efrian wondered how many would be left by nightfall. This thought led him to wonder if he was still in Nereus's good graces, for if not, surely his days, no, hours were also numbered.

***

The sun was hot, the day long, and as the end of the questioning was near, it became clear nothing was seen of Mabyn. Efrian started to relax. No one had reported him in town earlier, either.

Already, twenty-seven fae were unnecessarily sent to the garden of death to be mounted before nightfall. The men were weary. Suffocating heat-induced humidity added weakness and fear to the horror of upcoming deaths.

The last row stepped forward. Efrian recognized an older fae accompanied by his seven sons and their wives and children. On the right of the row, they took up more than half of the line. The old man's name was Vine Sines. He was an earth fae. His family had cultivated and managed the castle's vegetable gardens and fruit trees for years.

The Erlking started at the left end of the row and began to ask the same questions Efrian and the others had heard all day, and the answers remained the same.

"Have you seen Queen Mabyn?"

"No, Sir."

"Did you see any questionable characters go into or come from the castle yesterday?"

"No, Your Highness."

"Have you seen the guardsman, Saul, or the queen's chambermaid, Ova, in the last day or night?"

"No, my Erlking."

Efrian moved along in the listless nature of a sleepwalker. He heard Nereus's questions and the villagers' answers. He saw fear-filled faces. But he was cold to them now, although he knew echoes of the day were sure to haunt his dreams for many years to come.

One-third of the way down the line Efrian was swiftly awoken from this trance by the harsh voice of Nereus. "He is lying! Pull him from the line and secure him for the poles."

As two guards moved into action, Nereus shouted. "Cut off the heads of his wife and children!"

The guards did not hesitate as the fae unknown to Efrian pleaded for the Erlking's mercy. Each family member was pulled to the grass, laid face down, and a guard motioned to secure the fae with a foot to their back. Wails rode the early evening wind with each swing of the ax.

Efrian's eyes had wandered to the face under the mask. It lit the dwindled daylight as it pulsed with pain that was surely resonating through Nereus's body. The Erlking seemed to embrace the pain.

Guards dragged bodies to the cart and dumped them in with the twenty-eight fae headed for the poles. Efrian watched as Nereus continued down the line, stomping over bloody grass to get to the next victim. He could tell the Erlking was tired and greatly angered. There were still no witnesses to the escape of his queen.

Nereus pulled five fae from the line and without questioning ordered them to be taken to the dark garden. He stood in front of the old gardener and his family. The light under the Erlking's mask pulsed but its strength had diminished. Efrian's thoughts moved to the slaughter at the poles before them. His heart swelled for the swift way his kingdom had changed in a matter of months. If Famri had spoken the truth to the young guard in the castle halls earlier, the lands outside of the village were indeed drying up. How could Nereus let this happen? He thought of his wife and son and hoped they would be safe until he could join them.

"Vine Sines, step away from your family!" Nereus's voice pulled Efrian from his thoughts.

As a guard pulled the old man from the line, Nereus asked, "What have you seen?"

"I did not see anything, my Erlking, but we all woke late this morning. Felt like I had a head full of grog when I stumbled out of bed to have a quick breakfast before heading out to the castle gardens." The old man shook his head. "And shortly thereafter, I and my family heard your guards shouting Queen Mabyn was missing and everyone was to remain in their huts until notified. We complied, Your Highness." Vine Sines bowed his head.

"So, none of you saw anything?" the Erlking stared at the rest of the family.

Vine looked back at this family and nodded. One of the boys nodded back. The old man then turned back to the king. "Later, with the way I had felt after waking and my third son started to speak of the Queen's capture, I thought it was a dream, my Erlking. None of us was yet to have our morning nourishment. So when my third son stated, over a yawn, that he had seen Ova, the queen's chambermaid, and Efrian's wife and children, assorting Queen Mabyn out of the city, we all laughed, because as I have said, we woke late and we had just risen from our beds in a stupor."

"Are you saying your son's comment carries no validity?" Nereus screamed as two guards grabbed Efrian's arms.

"I believe so," the old man said. "We have known Efrian and his lovely wife, Jynifer, for many years. Why, I remember Efrian as a fledgling and—"

"Kill them all!" the king shouted.

The guards jumped to attention and began pulling Vine Sine's family to the ground. The little ones screamed and cried for their mothers.

"Stop!" Efrian shouted. "Do not kill them, Nereus, for it is true. My wife and children left the towns with Ova and Saul. They are hopefully alive in the Bad Lands. I had feared for their safety after your questioning of the guards last night."

Efrian bent to one knee. Nereus lifted a booted foot and kicked him backward, back to the ground. "Roll over!" Nereus shouted. "Guard!" Nereus motioned one of his men over. "Push him to the ground!"

With the Guard's boot on his back, Nereus stood over Efrian.

Efrian turned to look at Vine Sines. He smiled at the old man as Nereus swung the ax over his head. Efrian did not hear the screams of the townsfolk. He did not see the guards or the crowd even though his eyes were open. And he did not feel his head roll across the grass and stop at Vine Sines's feet.

CHAPTER EIGHTEEN

The Siege

Rampart slouched in the dark corner of the bar, sipping amber liquid from a cone rolled leaf. The poorly lit room housed several fae from the village outside the capital. Most sat on twig chairs, their shoulders hunched over the tables and their eyes focused on their cups. Light conversation murmured over the room, rarely rising above polite conversation levels. The usual laughter and singing found in fae bars was gone, replaced by trepidation. Rampart wore a glamour of an old man to hide from prying eyes, his face hidden behind wrinkles and a long white beard.

Dusk sat beside him, still in his invisible form. "I think this place is a bust," he said to Rampart softly. "I've been listening to every conversation since we got here. Lots of whining about life here in the outskirts, but I don't get the impression anyone is recruit material. They seem more eager to drink it away than do anything about it."

Rampart sighed. "Yeah, well, there's a few more places we can hit today before curfew. Still plenty of time to get some prospects for the rebellion."

Dusk shifted. Even though Rampart couldn't see him, he could tell the hellhound was agitated. "I'm not so sure about this," the hellhound said. "I don't think we're going to have luck today."

Rampart chuckled. "My friend, you've doubted us everyday, and yet we've made great contacts since we've been here. I know it's your nature to be a downer but try to have a little faith for once."

"I'm not being a 'downer,'" Dusk scoffed. "There's something not right here. I've sensed an unease, or a tension coarsening though the air."

Rampart sipped his drink. The liquid was sweet and tasted of apricot, but hit harder than any alcohol he drank before. Even the occasional sip was enough to send a tingling sensation up his throat and into his tongue. "You're just picking up on that now?" he said. "This town is full of people uprooted from their homes and made to live close to a madman who could order their execution if they look at him wrong. Can you blame them for being tense?"

"This is different. It's not just the misery of the people. Something has happened." Dusk lowered his voice even lower to the point it was almost a growl. "The townsfolk might not even be aware of it yet, but you know hellhounds are well attuned to detect negative energy. The last few hours I've been feeling it ramp up to the point the air feels thick with it. Something is brewing in the capital, and I don't think we want to be near it when it breaks."

It would have been easy for Rampart to write his warning off. Dusk was quick to spin stories of dread and caution, especially when he was bored. But there was an insistence in his voice that was difficult to ignore. "I'm not turning tail and running just because you have a bad feeling." Rampart finished his drink and set the empty cup on the table. "But you're right, this bar is a bust. Let's roam around a bit, see if we can gather some information." He slid his chair back and worked his way to the exit. None of the other patrons seemed to notice him. Then again, with the rate the majority of them sucked down their drinks, Rampart doubted anything less than a slap to the back of their head would be enough to get their attention.

The two of them walked out into the city street. This section of the town was comprised mostly of rudimentary structures the capital workers threw together in a hurry. The crude one room structures packed the streets in an unorganized fashion, and usually housed five or more families of fae. They functioned as little more than a place to sleep, as most of the tenants took to the streets during the day to avoid the crowded houses.

A group of kids ran past Rampart, laughing while chasing a pill bug desperately trying to get away from the excited children. Adults crowded campfires where they cooked and traded stories. A large grass woven basket with soapy water gathered several people washing clothes. They hung the wet laundry on lines strewn between buildings, making the streets seem even more crowded than they were.

The two of them wandered the streets, trying to avoid the commotion around them. Occasionally, Dusk would bump into someone, causing them to spin around in confusion. The wind coursed through the streets, catching a long white beard Rampart wore, tangling it into knots. He made a mental note not to wear this disguise on windy days.

As they walked, Rampart started to sense the unease in the people Dusk had described. Larger than normal groups crowded the streets, fae rushed from one group to another. There was a surge of anxiety through the streets he could feel more than see. Dusk was right; something definitely was up.

A young lady with purple skin and shiny silver wings moved to hurry past. Rampart jumped in front of her. "Excuse me, miss. Is there something going on in town? There seems to be a lot of commotion."

The fae stopped before crashing into him, her eyes wide. "Well, I don't know if it's true or not, just one of those things I heard from a friend who heard from a friend, but the rumor is the Erlking just executed his captain of the guard for treason."

Rampart stared at the young woman, trying to absorb what she said. "The captain... you mean Efrian?"

"Yeah, the guy who took over after Ozil. Like I said, though, it's been bad here. The Erlking questioning us, sending those before and after me to the poles. Still, people get anxious when news like this gets around because that tends to lead to stronger curfews and regulations. You know, all in the name of security they say, since the Queen disappeared."

Rampart nodded. "I know," he said in a daze. "Thank you." He moved out of the way to let the woman pass. She ran off presumably to find her family. Rampart stood on the street a moment before shuffling toward an empty alleyway. He placed his hand on the building wall and took a few deep breaths. He wasn't sure why, but he felt like someone punched him right in the diaphragm.

"Well, he certainly didn't last long, did he?" Dusk said from behind. "Guess he was a better soldier than he was a spy."

"The man did what he did while working as Nereus's right-hand man. What he did was amazing considering he was housed in the belly of the beast."

Dusk scoffed. "Wait, don't tell me you actually admire the guy. Just a few days ago you were ready to snap his neck on sight."

"It's complicated, Dusk," Rampart snapped. "Efrian did some unforgivable things, but like he said, we all did it in service of the Erlking. He could have been a great benefit to the rebellion given his position in the castle."

Dusk paused. "I don't think I'll ever understand this broad range of emotions you fae have. Bottom line is, the guy is dead and probably acting as a decoration for Nereus's death garden," he said plainly. "The question we have to worry about is whether or not he squealed on the rest of us before he met his end."

The hellhound's callousness drove Rampart to grit his teeth. "No way," he said. "And no, I'm not saying that out of faith. If Efrian had given up the resistance within the capital, we would have seen the guard mobilize long before the rumors of his death got anywhere near the town." Rampart peered down the alley way. The top of the castle loomed over the buildings. "But that lady was right, if Efrian was caught, there's no doubt going to be a crackdown on the capital. Nereus is a paranoid psychopath on a normal day. But if he found out yet another one of his captains has turned against him, he'll tear this town apart till he feels his bloodlust recede."

Dusk's paw prints dug into the dirt. "Then I think it's time we go with my original plan of getting the hell out of here, don't you think?"

Rampart nodded. "Hate to say it, but yeah. We can come back once things die down. We just have to make sure—"

Rampart was cut off by a woman's scream. Crashing and other commotion soon followed from the street where they just were. Several other voices shouted out. Rampart crept close along the wall and peeked out of the alleyway. He saw the same lady fae he had talked to being held on the ground by a guardsman. Six other guards stood over them, including one lieutenant. A man and a child were also being held back by the guard; the woman's family, Rampart guessed.

"If you have nothing to hide, why would you run from us?" the lieutenant shouted at her. "Anyone who refuses to be searched is automatically seen as a threat. If you cooperate, this will go much easier."

"Please," the woman begged, tears running down her face. "I wasn't running. Your men startled me, that's all."

The lieutenant sneered. "For your sake, I hope that's true. Load her up with the others for questioning. Her family, too, in case she needs incentive."

The other guards began ransacking the street. Overturning carts and laundry baskets. They kicked open house doors and pulled everyone into the streets. The other citizens stood still as statues, trying to avoid the guard's gaze. Next to the lieutenant, Rampart saw an orb hovering in the air about the size of his head. Inside it, purple smoke swirled with electricity pulsing through like a thunderstorm.

"Shit," Rampart mumbled while ducking back into the alley. "They have a Null."

"A what?" Dusk asked.

"A nullification sphere. It's a weapon made by the previous Erlking. They used it during the war to break through the veil and attack the jinn. It disrupts magic in an area around it, meaning if we get too close, my glamour won't work, and neither will your invisibility."

Dusk shifted back. "Then... let's not get close to it."

"Agreed. Let's get out of here."

The two of them headed down the alley, coming out the other side. Fae scrambled down the street. Crashing and the sound of guards' boots thudded on the dirt streets. It sounded like the guard was approaching from all sides. In the skies, the Erlking's guard hovered, making sure no one tried to escape their inspection through the air.

Rampart ducked down another alley as the guard crested the corner. The soldiers seemed to pour around every corner and marched every street. Rampart considered hiding in the buildings, but the one room houses would offer no place to hide from the guards.

He ran onto the next street where another wave of guards were searching. The lieutenant of this group was a woman he recognized from his days in the guard but couldn't remember her name. She stood half a block away, another null floating above her.

Rampart knew it was too close to him and Dusk. He felt his glamour collapse. The old man features melted away; his long beard shriveled up and disappeared. The fake faery wings darkened into his leathery imp wings. Dusk's cloak also failed, and the two stood exposed in the street.

Before they could react, the lieutenant turned her gaze to them. She narrowed her eyes. "Rampart!" she yelled, and the rest of her company turned toward them.

A wave of despair washed over him. It was the same feeling of hopelessness he felt as he watched the Copper Groves burn.

"Rampart!" Dusk yelled. "Follow me." The hellhound turned and ran back into the alley with Rampart and the guard following close behind. With a great bound, Dusk turned on a dime and tore through the building wall like tissue paper. Rampart grappled a line of laundry and tore it down as he followed, tangling up a guardsman a few steps behind. The chaos was enough to give them a little space from their grasp. Dusk busted through the opposite wall and into another building. This one housed a family in the process of being dragged out by a thin looking guard. Rampart shoulder checked him to the ground as he ran past.

The two continued dodging in and out of buildings, but every time they pulled away, they ran into more of the guard around each turn. The longer the chase continued, it became clearer to Rampart there wasn't an escape for him. Even if he somehow managed to evade them, they would never stop tearing the city apart looking for him. If he left, these people would suffer more. And he couldn't allow that.

"Go on ahead," he shouted to Dusk.

"Splitting up isn't a good idea," Dusk yelled over his shoulder. "If we're going to get out of here, it's going to take both of us."

"We're not getting out of here. You are." Rampart said. "They want me. They're not looking for you."

Dusk looked over his shoulder. "You're insane. Do you know what they'll do to you?"

"I have a good idea," he shouted as they rounded another corner. The guard closed in from behind. "But one of us has to get back to report to Coralina. And it sure as hell isn't going to be me."

Dusk hesitated.

"Go, you stupid mutt!" Rampart yelled. "We don't have time to argue."

Dusk looked back one more time before tearing around a corner. Rampart turned the other way. A few of the guard chased after Dusk, but nothing he couldn't lose. Most of the soldiers chased after Rampart, just like he thought. "Goodbye, my friend," he muttered to himself as he lost sight of the hellhound. His muscles burned, and his pursuers closed in. The running was over. But he couldn't give up without a fight.

He spun on his heel and buried his fist into the nearest guard's gut, right below his armor chest plate. The guard went down hard, but the wave behind quickly swarmed around and wrestled Rampart to the ground. They twisted his arms behind him and bound them to his wings with chains.

"Haul him up," the lieutenant ordered. As he was brought to his knees, Rampart saw her hovering over him with the Null hovering over the lieutenant's left shoulder, a smug look on her face. "Did you really think you'd be able to outrun us?"

"No, not really," Rampart huffed, looking at the surly faces surrounding him. "Can't blame a man for trying, though."

"Sure I can," she scoffed. "You've only made things worse for yourself."

"Worse for myself? Are you kidding?" In other circumstances, Rampart could have laughed.

"The man's got a point," a male voice came from behind them. The guard parted to show Famri approaching, wearing the captain's armor. "It really can't get worse for him," he said with a sneer.

This time, Rampart did laugh. "Famri, you're the new captain? Congrats man! All it took was for Ozil, me, AND Efrian to turn on the Erlking. Nereus must sleep soundly knowing his fourth pick is leading his men."

Famri scowled. "The three of you betrayed his trust, and the kingdom. So, yes, he can sleep soundly now knowing he finally has a captain he can trust and rely on." He clasped his hands behind his back and nodded to the surrounding guard. "I would die before turning my back on our king."

Rampart smiled. "Oh, I'm sure you would. Ever since I've known you, you've wanted nothing more than to be Nereus's right-hand puppet," he said. "Let me ask you, though, does he control you by strings or does he actually have to put his hand up your ass?"

Rampart had barely gotten the words out before Famri's boot connected with the side of his jaw. He collapsed in a heap; his vison blurred but never went black.

Famri leaned over him, a triumphant gleam crested his eye. "I know what you're doing," he said in a low voice.

"Yeah?" Rampart spat a clump of blood infused saliva on the ground. "And what would that be?"

"You're hoping you can anger me enough to kill you before we can interrogate you for information."

Rampart chuckled. "Oh, yeah that would probably have been smart, wouldn't it?" he said. "But, honestly, I'm just trying to piss you off. How's it working?"

Famri sneered and straightened his back. "Bring him to his feet," he barked at his soldiers.

Strong hands wrapped around Rampart's arms and pulled him upright. Once he was on his feet, Rampart could see he was surrounded by no less than twenty guard members. Civilians lined the street, some looked on with curiosity, but most stood with their heads down, too scared to walk away while the guard was present.

"Search him," Famri commanded. The lieutenant began patting Rampart down and poking her fingers in his pockets.

"What are you hoping to find?" Rampart asked with a raised eyebrow.

"You didn't come to the capital for a holiday," Famri said as he observed the inspection. "You were here to spread your venomous words against our king. I want names of those you could have turned to your cause."

"And you think I would write these names on a list and carry them around in my pockets?" Rampart laughed. "How stupid do you think I am?"

The lieutenant finished her search and shook her head at her captain.

Famri sighed. "I guess that would have been too easy, but it doesn't matter." He stepped closer. "You would save yourself a lot of grief if you would simply tell me where your traitorous cell is located within the

capital. Then you would be spared the need for the Erlking's more...
advanced interrogation."

Rampart wore a thin smile. "Oh, I'm sure you'd love to present that
to him. You'd earn quite a favor from your king with that information,
wouldn't you?" Rampart leaned forward. "Let me be as clear as I can for
that small brain of yours. I'd rather have my eyes peeled out of my skull
layer by layer from a flesh-eating bacterium before I help you gain more
clout with the Erlking. There is no threat you can whisper, or pain you
could administer, that would make me give you any information about
the rebellion."

Famri narrowed his eyes before a smile creased the corners of his
mouth. "Oh, it sounds like the Erlking will have his fun with you.
You'll tell him everything, and when you're drained and on the brink
of death, he'll drag your limp and broken body before the entire capital
to witness your execution. I can only hope our great and wise king
will grant me the killing blow myself." With that, he spun on his heel.
"Bring him. And Lieutenant, continue your search."

The two guards at Rampart's side grasped his arms tightly and
followed their captain toward the castle. Sorrowful eyes watched as
they marched past the civilians. Rampart could only hope Dusk
managed to get out of the capital. If he managed to bring word to
Coralina of the capital rebels, then all of this wouldn't be nothing.

CHAPTER NINETEEN

An Undeniable Death Threat

Rampart sat with his back to a cold rock wall. Famri had brought him directly to the cell his comrade Ozil had been detained in before he and Abdul had rescued him. The view from the inside was different. His arms in chains, the likelihood of him getting out alive was a given.

Famri had dismissed the rest of the guard immediately when they arrived at the castle and had taken it upon himself to imprison him. Rampart was sure Famri did not want an audience when he told Nereus he had not only captured one of the leaders of the revolution but had him in chains for the Erlking's viewing pleasure.

A smile spread across the imp's lips, and he tucked his grey wings tighter behind his back. Silver hair fell over a bare chest and covered the tattoos on his arms. His stormy eyes sparkled. Famri had no clue of the pleasure he had taken from the king. Nereus would have loved to push Rampart down the stairs, feet shackled and arms secured behind his back as he stumbled into a cell.

The only things Famri had accomplished correctly were to be close when his guard had captured the imp, and the order he gave the guard not to tell anyone of the prisoner. Famri had threatened them. He said that if Rampart's capture got around before the Erlking could surprise the town with it, Famri himself would arrest the guardsmen for treason right in front of the Erlking. Problem was that the people had already witnessed it. Another blunder that would have a surprise ending for the idiot.

Rampart sighed. "Yet here I am," he told no one, his voice hollow in the depths of the dungeon. He bent his legs and rested his forehead on his knees, arms wrapped around his legs. At least the chains allowed him to sit.

"I will accept my life's end and never utter a word," he mumbled. "But hear me now all that is winged in heaven," his gruff voice shouted as he raised his eyes to the ceiling. "It is my dying wish that Coralina does not blame herself. My demise must not be on her. I wanted to come here! I wanted talk to the guard myself!"

Rampart heard a chuckle and fought an urge to turn in that direction. Dusk trotted out of the darkness.

"I told you to go warn the others," Rampart scolded.

"Yeah, and I heard you, but I hung around. No one paid attention to my cute, little, black pup disguise."

"And the Null?"

Dusk snorted. "It never got close."

"Why are you here?" Rampart said. "Do you want to watch me die?"

"I won't deny a death wish has crossed my mind on occasion." The sides of Dusk's maw turned up in a doggy smile. "But that's not why I'm here.

"I was headed out of town as you asked and trotted right into Saul. You remember Saul. The guard Mabyn's chamber maid had the hots—"

"That's enough," Rampart warned. "I remember him."

Dusk laid down, back legs tucked under his rump, front paws stretched out before him. "He told me Coralina and the rest of the caravan were no longer safe. The Bad Lands are rapidly expanding, and trees are no longer blinds for safe travel. Saul said talk among the guard was swiftly turning toward the king holding their families in the hive for ransom, not for their well-being. The men not only fear for their wives and children's lives but their own.

"There is a movement against the king, a small one, but the numbers are growing. Saul said the guards exchanged rumors. One of them heard Nereus knew where Coralina would leave the Bad Lands to head toward the castle." Dusk snorted. "Hell, all he has to do is send a few hive wasps to watch the gate along the perimeter.

"Also, after Nereus's men came back from the hive there was news of a portal from Hell right by the hive. They spoke of the creatures that popped out. Supposedly that's when chatter amongst the guards became more frantic, and guards became more diligent about listening in on Nereus's orders."

Rampart stood. "Do we know whether Nereus has sent any wasps or guards to the hive recently?"

"No. And that's why Saul said I should move the caravan to the caves under Copper Groves. He said the rivers had run deep there and may still be moist. Maybe even a few small puddles. I personally think we need to get the guards' families out of that hive, too."

"We can't take that chance."

"Screw that!" Dusk said. "Here's what I think. Cal needs to contact Abdul and give the jinn a wake-up call. Things are moving fast. The jinn can open The Gray. I'll help him lead the caravan to the caves. Then we can go back for the fae in the hive."

Rampart inhaled through his nose and blew air out his mouth. "Fine. But hear this, under no circumstances is anyone to attempt my rescue. Right now, I'm the only deterrent for Nereus. Move swiftly. Do you understand? No one comes back here. And watch out for the Nulls."

Dusk used his front paws to push himself into a sitting position and lifted a back paw. He licked the pads under his foot and then scratched his left ear with it. The hellhound stood, turned in a circle, and shook. He slowly moved to face Rampart. "On my way out of town, I'll tell Saul the plan and ask him to join us in the Bad Lands today with any of the king's guard that wishes to join us," he said as he started toward the stairway.

"Did you hear everything I said?" Rampart asked.

"I did," he said, and with a sidewards glance, the hellhound continued. "The part about abandoning you doesn't sit well. I was thinking—"

Rampart grabbed the metal bars of the cell and squeezed until his knuckles turned white. "Don't think. Get the hell out of here and tell Coralina my last words were that she is not to blame herself for my death. And tell Abdul my dying wish was to save her and the others. You guard the caves with Mabyn, Reka, and Ozil. Thanks to Saul, we know where the guards' families are being held. The Watcher and Abdul can fly to the hive and bring them to the safety of the caves with the others. Coralina will do the rest."

"You already owe Abdul one wish," Dusk barked. "What makes you think he'll grant a dead man another?"

"You're trying my patience, Hellhound! Get the hell out of here and let me die in peace or I'll wish you back to Hell where you belong."

Dusk's eyes turned red; his hair stood on end. His body started to fade. "I'll grant you this but I don't like it." His voice faded as he climbed the stairs.

Rampart sat down, wings to the wall, again. He hung his head and closed his eyes. "Now I wait," he whispered.

The silver-haired half-breed's head slumped as his eyes closed and thoughts of the past led to a dream of the future. He saw Coralina sitting on the throne, alone in a moonlit room, tears running down her cheeks. A whisper escaped her lips, "I should have never suggested he go..."

Rampart's head shot upward. "It was not your fault, Coralina! I chose to come here! Me. Not you! And I now choose to die here."

"Excellent!" Nereus's voice came from above, followed by the heavy footsteps of his guard. He jovially said, "So, you're ready to die, are you? I can't wait to watch you gasp for that last breath. I will be sure all spectators know Coralina sent you to your death, not their king. And I will have a special banner hung around your neck defaming her name until the raptors color it with your blood and shred it to use for their nests. But first, we must talk."

Nereus came to stand before the cell; heaven's fire fought for Rampart's attention from under the king's hideous leather mask. But he was drawn to the Erlking's eyes as they flickered with another light, demented and lustful amusement.

"Where is my wife? Are Reka and Ozil in the Bad Lands?" When there was no answer, Nereus shouted, "Has the illegitimate bitch called her Watcher to round up heaven and hell for her cause?

"Listen to me, Rampart. I know you are half-bred, but you proved yourself to me. You were one of my favorite guards. If we were to neuter you, I could give you charge of my men. That weakling Famri is useless, not to mention his misaligned greed to please me. Do you hear me? Just say the word and I will set you free. Right now."

Rampart stared at the wall in front of him for a heartbeat, then closed his eyes.

"I need this, damn you!" the Erlking said. "I see my realm falling from my grace, my guard watching with fear instead of admiration." He paused and paced on the other side of the bars. "Although fear is a palpable delight in most situations it is not welcomed within my guard. I've learned over the years, fear bleeds like rot in a bowl of fruit. It leads to betrayal. It weakens the brain and, in turn, the magic that makes us the creatures we were born to be. And like a bowl of fruit, the rotted must be culled, the remainder cleaned and cared for, and the discarded replaced. I can replace Famri with you."

Rampart stretched his legs out, yawned, and put his palms on the fetid rock below him. He closed his eyes, pushed his rear end closer to the wall, and made no attempt to glance in the Erlking's direction.

"Look at me," Nereus warned.

Rampart did not concentrate on what was before him, or the rumbling in his stomach and bowels. Instead, he thought of Coralina. If all went well, she would be sitting on the throne of her people, not this horrid man on the other side of the bars. He could easily take death for that. He took deep soothing breaths, tuned out the king's words that droned on and on, and still, fear roiled inside his body.

"...and I will start plucking one family from the hive daily, have them killed, Rampart, without the slightest regret. LOOK AT ME!"

Rampart tried to visualize Coralina's smartass grin in the purple haze behind his eyelids and drown out the king's words with the sound of her laughter. His bowels rumbled and he leaned sideways and expelled the built-up gasses.

Nereus grabbed the cell door and shook it. "You son of an imp! GUARDS! Drag this shitter out of the cell and bring the cart around. He's going to die before night shoves itself up the arse of another day."

Rampart heard the Erlking's words, and Coralina's amused vision faded. He felt saddened that he would never see her again. But for the first time, Rampart knew the Erlking's rein was about to end. He was proud he had taken a part in it. After Ozil's escape, Efrian's death, and now his capture, the townsfolk were sure to rebel, and the guard would follow, especially when they realized their families were not being held safely for their dedication, but to use against their rebellion in the coming days. His mind flashed with visuals of the townsfolk he was too busy to assess during his capture. They were mutely terrorized, moving like the dead come alive, slow and empty. There was irreparable damage to this king's empire. It was time to remove Nereus before there was nothing left to emancipate them from the shackles of his tyranny. It was time for Coralina.

***

The sun was struggling to rise. The air was thick with the smell of blood, and the fae still wandered the streets. As a horn blew, signaling the Erlking's arrival, some scattered to alleys, others to their homes.

Nereus shouted, "We have a traitor; once a guardsman, but now a close ally of Coralina, my illegitimate daughter who wants my throne!"

A crowd reluctantly began to gather around the guards that were almost unnoticeably slow to raise their fists and react with boos and the harsh words the king was looking for. Rampart's fellow guardsmen looked akin to weak and abandoned fledglings on their way to the human world to be exchanged for healthy changelings brought back for breeding hundreds of years ago. A bare-chested fae with dark skin and a large yellow snake imbedded into his skin and face viewed the Erlking through the snake's eye. Behind the snake man, Rampart thought he saw Saul, surrounded by guardsmen, their wings spread over armor, swords at their hips. They all had crossbows over their shoulders. Rampart's brow furrowed, his eyes a watery blur from the tightness of the rope around his throat.

When the noose was removed a few minutes later, his vision slowly cleared. As he was pushed down and his cheek hit the ground, the Erlking's axman moved forward. Saul's eyes locked on Rampart's, and a smile formed on his face. The whole scene felt surreal to the imp as he tried to shake his head.

Nereus's words cut the air and reality fell hard on Rampart's back with the boot of the axman. "We will cut off Rampart's head and send it to Coralina with a message!"

The Erlking's face flamed with the Watcher's fire on one side, the other raked in flickering shadow under flashing blue eyes: a king from the depths of hades blinding the dusk of the waning night. "We know where Coralina and her weak, meek, minimal followers are. We will kill them off as if they were fireflies in a lidded jar. She sent this imp fae, half breed to kill me and my guard."

A large crowd had formed and Nereus definitely had their attention. "Before they hurt our realm and my vision for a clean new Faery Lands, I will destroy all of them."

"I was not sent here to kill you!" Rampart shouted. "I was sent to tell you the guards' families are safe with us in the Bad Lands!" He prayed that was true.

"Blasphemy! This is not true!" Nereus shouted.

The ax-guard pressed his booted foot down hard on Rampart's back, his eyes on Nereus. Nereus raised his hand, and the guard raised his ax. All eyes moved to the ax.

The Erlking, face aflame, eyes capturing Rampart's, shook his hand, teasing, dragging out his death. Arm still raised, Nereus stepped closer to the axman and turned his right arm to the crowd. "Are you ready?"

Rampart stared up at the king and forced a smile.

The angel fire under the mask billowed from the edges of the mask as the Erlking whispered, "I want to watch the blood pour out of your body and soil the grass, and the light of your life drain from your eyes until they turn milky white. I will smile when your chest deflates with your last breath."

"Go ahead and kill me then!" Rampart yelled. "Because my death will be the end of yours as well."

The Erlking lowered his arm, and before the axman could follow his cue, six arrows flew over the silent crowd and slid into the axman's back. All six tore into his heart. Blood spewed from his nostrils and mouth as the axman slowly dropped to his knees and fell sideways. He hit the ground next to Rampart and one arm fell over Rampart's chest as if trying to hold the imp captive. The ax hit the ground hard, inches from Rampart's head, kicking up dirt and grass.

Rampart and Saul exchanged a look.

Guards surrounded Nereus, wings flapping as they carried him off toward the cart.

Fourteen guards, led by Saul, shot into the air, wings buzzing, armor clanking.

Rampart shoved the axman off his body, jumped up, and spread his wings. He looked into the crowd and yelled, "We got this! I will be back!" and flew above the townsfolk to catch up with Saul and the guards. Two more small groups of guards cheered and shot into the sky to join Saul.

Rampart's gray, leathery wings buzzed like a hummingbird as he hovered over the field. He shot a stream of fire at Nereus. It did nothing but light a flaming path behind the fast-moving cart but it made him smile.

CHAPTER TWENTY

Calm Before the Storm

Coralina gazed into the deep blackness of the cave. Cold air wafted upward from the darkness, chilling the sweat beaded on her forearms. "We won't be able to get the wagons through there," she said. "But if it runs as close to the capital as you say, that's fine. The soldiers will go on foot and the caravan can wait here, either for the news of victory, or the retreat of survivors."

"I believe Saul," Dusk said, pacing the entrance of the cave. "We'll be able to get the families safe and to the caravan and get our people in striking position. I tell you; this is your best chance of getting to the capital city without raising alarm."

Coralina refused to let her eyes shift toward the hellhound. His plan was sound, she had to admit, but her anger toward Dusk was still too raw to give the hound acknowledgement. Instead, she crossed her arms and stubbornly kept her gaze forward. "A task that would be easier if I was going in with one of my top lieutenants at my side."

Even without looking, she could feel Dusk's eyes piercing into her. "Rampart was very clear on what he wanted," he said in a low deep voice. "You know how stubborn he can be when he's made up his mind."

"And I know how stubborn you can be as well," she shot back. "With all those powers you speak of having, you really don't think you could've been able to get him out of there?"

"Do you really think I left him there so callously?" he said in a low growl. "Rampart was sure his course of action was the right one, and not even I could drag him out of there kicking and screaming. He's bound and determined to see the Erlking fall, and for you to take the throne. Even if that means his life is to be sacrifi—"

Dusks words cut off as Coralina dragged the air from his lungs with a twist of wrist. It was a reactionary move she immediately regretted, but she couldn't hear that word right now. As Dusk gasped, she let the breath flow back into lungs. "Don't say things like that till there is reason to," she said as calmly as she could. "Afterall, Nereus kept Ozil alive after his capture to savor his victory; he might do the same with Rampart."

Coralina expected an explosion of anger from the hellhound, but none came. Instead, he gave a breathy scoff that sent dust swirling from the ground. "We can always hope, but I'm not well known for my optimism." The hound turned. "I'll let that little tantrum of yours slide this time, potential queen, due to the circumstances. But keep in mind, I owe you nothing. What I do for you I do under my own volition, and I can be a powerful ally to you. But if crossed, my bite is most certainly worse than my bark." With that, he turned and walked toward the caravan, his paws thumping on the dried ground.

With Dusk gone, her anger turned inward. She knew there were risks when she sent Rampart to the capital, and what would happen if he got caught. But somehow, she never thought he'd get caught. Rampart had been through impossible situations before and escaped them with hardly a scratch. It was as if he had a shield of invulnerability that kept him safe. It blinded Coralina to the risks they took every time they went to battle or behind enemy lines, which made it easier to assign him to dangerous missions. But in the back of her mind, Coralina feared this day would come. A day when he wouldn't return, and she didn't know how to quell the anger boiling within.

She gazed into the cave and found comfort in the darkness dwelling beyond the rocks. The empty nothingness was welcoming as she stood amongst the ruins of the Copper Groves clan. Burned buildings and fallen treehouses littered the ground behind her, like looming ghosts of a previous failure. Coralina couldn't help but wonder, would there be anything left of the fae, even if they won? Was there any other choice?

A rustling from behind broke through her thoughts. She turned to see Broka hurrying toward her, huffing and puffing. "Coralina, I have a report," he said through breaths. He doubled over. "I should have flown here, but no, Aoeife told me I had to stay low in case—"

"—Broka!" Coralina snapped. "I'm not in the mood for your complaining. Just tell me what you need and leave me alone."

The gargoyle jumped. "Oh, sorry. Complaining is just in my nature, but honestly this time I bring good news, for a change."

Coralina raised an eyebrow.

"Our scouts came back from the settlement around the castle, and they said there's been a revolt amongst the guards. The streets are in complete chaos. The guard is being pushed back toward the capital as they try to figure out who is still loyal."

Coralina stood motionless as the information soaked in. It was a scenario that played out so many times in her head that it felt like fiction. "That's... incredible! Do they know what sparked that?"

Broka paused. "The Erlking gathered the town for Rampart's execution. But before it was carried out, all hell broke loose."

Coralina's heart skipped a beat. "Did they save him? Did they get him out of there?"

"I... they, don't know for sure," he said. "The scouts saw the Erlking taken from the stage, but lost sight of Rampart after that. Things broke down fast. They hurried to get here and report."

Coralina let out an audible sigh, comforted by the hope Rampart was able to get away. "This is the perfect time then." She put her hand on his shoulder and turned him around. "Come on, back to camp. It's time to round up the troops."

They hurried back to where the caravan was hidden. The wagons were parked under fallen structures that once were the buildings of the Copper Grove clan. The burnt bones of the city kept their camp from the patrol's eyes, but also harbored an aura of sadness. Not too long ago, this city was the symbol of the resistance, a foothold against the Erlking's guard, and home to many friends. Coralina could still hear the drums and flutes from their celebrations wafting in the air, and see their delicate bodies dancing around campfires if she closed her eyes.

Half fae scampered between buildings, running supplies between the wagons. Ozil stood in the open, directing the traffic. His armor shined in the sun, a product of polishing it daily. It was a habit he kept from the days as guard captain, even though Coralina would tease him for it. 'Respect your armor, respect your life,' he would always respond. She always wondered if that was his own motto, or one drilled into his brain from the guard.

"You didn't waste any time readying the troops, did you, Captain?" Coralina said with a smile.

"Of course not," Ozil said with clasped hands behind his back. His eyes darted back and forth, keeping an eye on the proceedings. "It's my job to anticipate your orders and prepare for them."

Coralina watched a wheelbarrow full of swords and shields be pushed at a dangerous speed between the buildings. Every bump sent them clanging against each other and threatened to bounce from the container. "Given what I'm seeing, it seems you're assuming I'll order a full out assault on the castle."

Ozil raised an eyebrow. "Are you not?"

Coralina laughed. "Of course I am, but I can't help but wonder if the half fae are ready. They've only just begun to unlock their true potential; do you think it's enough?"

Ozil shrugged. "If my many years of experience has taught me anything, it's battles rarely come at convenient times. Sometimes you just got to take the opportunities you're given. What I do know is we're being granted a golden opportunity to act, and if we don't take it now we may never get another chance."

Coralina nodded. "Alright, so with your many years of experience, tell me. How exactly do we go about attacking the castle?"

"Good question," a voice said from behind. Coralina turned to see Cal and Aldul walking up on them. Cal's wings draped over his shoulders. The one made from smoke dripped gold and green tendrils. "I mean, do we have a plan here?" Cal asked.

Ozil didn't seem to notice their approach as his gaze continued to watch over the preparations. "I am the plan," he said. "With the revolt, the whole area will be in chaos. We won't know exactly what we're walking into till we get through the cave. Then I can lead our troops through the streets. There isn't anyone in our camp or the guard that knows the city better than I do. I was guarding it longer than most of them have been alive."

Cal laughed. "I guess the rest of us can just hang back. Ozil's got this."

Ozil rolled his eyes. "Hardly. Our attack will draw out the majority of the guard, and that will open the way for you three and the other jinn forces to infiltrate the castle and take down Nereus."

Coralina crossed her arms. "I'm surprised, Captain. I thought you'd want to be a part of the team to haul his ass off his throne."

"Want? Yes, of course I would. But my people come first, and our troops need me more than you do. And with any luck, we'll find Rampart there alive and well with more soldiers at his side." A sparkle of pride lit Ozil's eye. "The two of us would be quite a force for the guard to recon with."

"For all his flaws, the Erlking is no fool," Aldul said. "How can you be sure he won't merely tighten his forces around the castle?"

Ozil chuckled. "Two of his former guard leaders turn up at his doorstep brandishing swords against him, both who had at one time been captured and escaped his clutches. Nereus will be salivating at the chance to publicly end us. Besides, it would be a further embarrassment to him if we marched so close to his castle, just to slip through his fingers again." Ozil shook his head. "He'll send his troops, trust me. And when he does your strike team of jinn will have an opening to storm the castle. The confusion within should give you a shot at taking the bastard down."

Cal fidgeted, scratching the back of his head. "I mean, it's not a bad plan. It's just..." His eyes bounced between the three of them. "If this doesn't work, that's it, game over. The half fae are powerful, but still vastly outnumbered by the guard. Even with you, and hopefully Rampart, at the helm there's still going to be many losses. And if Nereus slips away—"

"Then it's all over anyway," Coralina interrupted. "We all knew it would come to this in the end. We've been biding time waiting for the right time. And this is the best shot we have. If we miss, either Nereus will keep his rule or the fae world will fall to ruin." She smiled at him. "Still glad you came back?"

Cal laughed. "I don't know about 'glad,' but I'm not going anywhere. Curious to see how all this ends now, and absolutely would like another shot at Nereus." He extended his hand, a bright white flame the size of a baseball erupted in his palm. "I've been practicing with holy fire. I'm still not exactly proficient with it, but I've gained more control of the flame. Enough to give Nereus another handprint if he doesn't stand down."

"He won't," Coralina said. "He'd die before giving up the throne."

The statement made Cal look uncomfortable. His smile dimmed and his eyes darted as he thought. "I mean, that might very well be true. But if by chance he does surrender, we'd take it right?"

The other three turned their attention to the angel. Even Ozil took his eye off the preparations.

"Cal, after all this, don't tell me you're getting cold feet." Coralina said. Her voice dropped into her authoritative tone she'd been practicing. "You don't leave a man like that alive. Do you know how dangerous that would be? I mean, what are you going to do, lock him in his own prison? As amusing as I would find seeing him in chains, Nereus is too powerful to simply lock away. More than that, the guard won't accept me as their queen till he's either dead or passed his authority to me, which he'll never do of his own free will. Then after all this, we'll end up still fighting each other."

Cal sighed and nodded. "I know where you're coming from. And I agree with you, but if he surrenders—"

"I told you, he won't," Coralina said. She flexed her jaw. "Freaking angels, how long is it going to take you to realize things work differently in this world? You can't always reason your way out of situations. There's no happy ending where we sit down and have tea with Nereus and sort out an ending where he isn't in charge. This is our reality. It's dark, painful, and full of blood and tears. But it is what it is. You understand?"

Cal's expression softened. "It is what it is," he repeated. "Perhaps that's something a future queen could help improve, eh?"

Coralina paused. She had expected more resistance from him. "Perhaps," she said. She had been so focused on the war, she hadn't actually thought about what she would do if she won. But Cal was right; as the new Erlking, she would have the power to shape this world, just like Nereus did before her. Except, hopefully, for the better.

***

"How dare they attack me!" Nereus's rage infused voice bounced off the stone walls of the throne room. "My own people, in my own city! It's humiliating, and everyone was there to see it!"

Nereus's feet thudded against the carpet. He was flanked on both sides by his twin advisors, Thallia and Diaspor. Behind trailed Famri, cautiously walking as to not fall behind, but also not draw too near to the fuming Erlking.

"We should consider a rational response," Thallia said, her voice calm and soothing in contrast to the Erlking's fury.

"Rational?!" Nereus spun on his heel and poked his finger into Thallia's chest. "You and your brother have been preaching that shit since I was crowned. Where has that gotten us? No, I'm going to show these people a completely irrational response. No one will dare raise so much as a voice to me after the horrors I unleash upon these traitors."

"With all due respect," Diaspor said before he was cut off by Nereus raising his hand for silence.

"It has been long since these halls have heard proper respect being spoken," Nereus spat. "And I've heard enough spinless advice."

Famri's blood turned cold as Nereus eyes turned to him. The Erlking snarled and stepped closer. "And what kind of captain are you?!" he yelled. "I saw your men among the dissidents, shooting arrows at me. Have you lost complete control of your soldiers?"

Famri tried to hide his panic. He knew one wrong response could mean his death. He'd seen the Erlking execute guardsmen on a whim for no other reason than to calm himself. Famri knew he couldn't point out how he had just taken over the position, because Nereus would view it as an excuse. In his eyes, Famri, as captain, was responsible for everything the guard did, good and bad.

"It seems Efrian's weak leadership was infectious to his underlings," Famri said with a shaky voice. "I'll find the traitors and bring them and their families before you. Their executions will strengthen the others' resolve."

Famri hoped matching the Erlking's ruthlessness would quell his rage. Nereus's jaw clenched and Famri swore he could feel his blood being pulled from within. But, ultimately, the king scoffed and turned his back.

"Traitors everywhere," Nereus murmured as he walked toward his throne. "Ozil, Efrian, guardsmen, citizens." His voice escalated as the list grew. "My own queen and daughter! My throne has been surrounded by betrayers and weakness for too long! We must cleanse this evil before it spreads further."

Outside the castle walls, an explosion erupted, big enough the castle floors vibrated under their feet.

"And your will shall be done," Thallia said. "But first, our attention should be focused on your safety, my lord. The fighting in the city may seem trivial, but any insurgents this close to the castle may pose a threat." She gave Famri a side glance with glassy eyes. "Especially if there is concern of the loyalty of your guard."

Famri's blood boiled. Had they not been in the presence of the Erlking, he would have drawn his sword on the aging fae. Instead, he clasped his hands behind him and calmed his breaths. "There is no doubt of loyalty; the guard is behind their king," Famri said. "What happened at Rampart's execution was nothing but a few misguided fools left from the old regime. They will be found and punished."

Nereus ascended the staircase to his throne. "See that they are, Captain," he said, swinging himself onto the chair. "Bring the traitors and misguided fools to the castle, stake them to the ground lining the entrance, and surround them with their families' heads on spikes. They can starve to death watching the skin of their loved ones rot. If there is space left, fill it with random civilians. People will believe their guilt if we say they're guilty."

Famri bowed his head. "I will see it done."

Nereus raised a bony finger. "This is your moment. If you succeed with this task, when we defeat Coralina, you will forever be known as the captain who was at my side when we quelled the evil of this land. You'll forever be known as a great hero of our kingdom." The Erlking leaned back on his throne and smiled. "Fail, and you'll join the long line of disappointing captains, and meet their same fate."

Famri stretched his arms in respect and backed out of the room, closing the large wood doors behind him.

Diaspor smiled, brushing long white strands of hair from his face. "The young captains always amuse me, so eager to please, so naïve."

Nereus sighed. "They haven't been the same since Ozil. These younger ones lack the nobility needed to be a true captain of the guard. Dreams of glory drive them forward, but they lack in abilities. Rampart was probably the closest to being a worthy successor. Shame he was born with such impurities," he said, picking at his blue robes. "It's almost lucky Rampart lives. I feel we could do something more... creative with his execution. Perhaps we could make him and Ozil fight to the death; that could prove entertaining."

Diaspor fluttered his thin transparent wings. "Speaking of your former captains," he said with the same soothing tone as his sister. "Do you worry they may try to take advantage of the turmoil in the city and attack?"

Nereus waved his hand. "Worry, no, of course not. After all, we've spent much time and effort trying to force them into making an incursion." The Erlking laughed from his belly. "Hell, maybe this will be a good thing. If they do come then all our enemies will be in one place. We can wipe them out finally, and I can turn my attention to other lands. The jinn, of course, will need to pay for their involvement with the rebels. But we don't have to worry about that right now."

Thallia glanced at the wooden doors at the end of the hall. "You have faith this new captain has the wit about him enough to stop Coralina?"

"Faith has nothing to do with it, my advisor." Nereus sneered. "He still commands an army of guardsmen that dwarfs the numbers the rebels have amassed. They have journeyed far to get here. They are starving, tired, and weak. Even Coralina has enough awareness to know they can't win a prolonged battle."

Thallia thought for a moment and turned toward Nereus with her hands clasped behind her back. "Still, there could be a danger to you," she said. "We should take the escape tunnels and hide you till this is over."

A twinkle shinned in Nereus's right eye. "No. I won't be chased from my castle, certainly not by my own daughter." He growled before showing a toothy grin. "You forget, dear advisors, the most powerful deterrent we have to the rebels ... is me."

CHAPTER TWENTY-ONE

Nereus screamed at Famri, "I want as many of my guardsmen inside this castle as possible, and soon! And you better make sure they are the most loyal. Take the rest and wait for whatever is headed our way after you deal with getting the families back. I am sure there will be an attempted takeover. I feel my best option is to defend from the inside and use the families as a wall of protection with the rest of the guards outside. You will lead the guardsmen outside the castle after you do as told. The first six guardsmen that show any sign of dishonor are to be murdered on the spot and in front of the others. Then pile them up at the front gate. That is sure to keep those weak half-bred fools from thinking they can overpower me!"

Famri bolted out the castle doors and nodded at his guardsmen as he approached the gates. One of the fae immediately stepped forward to let him through.

"May the sovereign's strength be with you, Sir," the guardsman said, head bowed as Famri passed.

Without giving his usual response, 'And also with you', Femri gritted his teeth and increased his steps to a hair's breadth under a run and headed for town.

"Strength, my arse!" Famri panted, his anger pushing him faster. "Our Sovereign's manic frenzy of murder, mayhem, and intimidation will soon drain our people as swiftly as the water drains from our lands," he grumbled, boots creating dust clouds around his black trousers. "Nereus has brought a mighty curse on us all. And yet, I obey his commands and suffer an anxiety-ridden post just to walk by his side. If

I disobey now, I'm sure to become another head in his garden of hell. I should kill him myself and take his seat. I'd be a much better ruler than he."

Famri's arms pumped to the beat of his feet, and spittle flew from his mouth with each angry word. "So, Sire, who shall I frivolously maim and murder for you today? That of the first guards I see upon entering their quarters? Perhaps I shall also send them to the hive to collect their wives and children first. Yes! That should please the bastard on the throne and light up his face like one hundred torches gathered from the halls of his castle."

***

"Did everything go as planned?" Ozil asked.

Saul smiled with admiration and trust for his old captain. "Yes, Sir, and before we went to the hive to collect the families, Rampart and I removed Efrian's body from the Dark Garden. Rampart used his magic and we put Efrian's ashes in a small pottery urn for his wife. She was thankful, but still taking her husband's death pretty hard, Sir. We were grateful for the comfort the other families gave as we moved toward Copper Groves."

"I will personally pay my respect as soon as I see her," Ozil said. "Did you stay to see no one showed animosity toward the guards' families, and all were safely settled with the caravan?"

"They are secure," Saul said, "and were warmly welcomed. Everyone is saddened by the loss of Efrian."

Ozil sighed. "Yes, and so they should be. Without his love for our people, we would not be facing off with the Erlking today. I'm sure his sacrifice added even more to our numbers. I will personally see to it that Jynifer and Jaris wear the amulet of Eternal Safety and Respect among the people of Faery Lands for his deeds. Even though that, in my opinion, isn't enough. He gave his life for our strength to see this through. I will talk to Coralina when she sits on the throne. His family name must be etched in the book of our realm's history as the fae that saved our kingdom from the monster that ruled it for way too long.

"I am pleased, and eternally grateful you and Rampart removed Efrian and delivered his ashes to Jynifer." Ozil patted Saul on the back. "An excellent show of leadership."

Standing next to Saul, Dusk grunted. Neither fae paid notice.

Chatter rode the wind rustling the trees ahead and both men slowed down. They were close to the open field behind the villages.

Ozil shoved a hand under his helmet and scratched. "I assume Rampart will join us in town later?"

"No," Saul said.

"Oh?" Ozil looked up at his guard. "Coralina then?"

Dusk's throat rumbled with a stifled growl. Again, both fae paid him no mind.

"I'm not sure what Coralina's plans are going to be," Saul answered. "But Rampart told me he was going to leave the guardsmen's families under the protection of Mabyn, and he'd be back here to meet me in town as soon as he spoke with Coralina. He wants me to help him guide the townsfolk to Copper Groves."

"Excellent!" Ozil said with a grin. "With the queen's powers, the guardsmen's families are safe. I'm sure she will have everyone settled deep within the tunnels under the city."

"I agree," Saul said. "You know, the Erlking's jealous stupidity by not allowing Mabyn her rightful place in the guard was his first mistake."

"Probably so," Ozil agreed. "Having seen her skills firsthand, I'm sure Mabyn was a threat to his strength and power. She would have never obeyed him."

"I'd love to see her in battle," Saul said.

"So you might, but I'm afraid for now it's just you and me," Ozil stated. "If you were single-handedly able to round up a crew to rescue

Rampart, I'm sure, together, we can gather enough guardsmen to back up Coralina's arrival."

Saul nodded. "Hopefully. We must swiftly establish who is with us and who is not before Rampart gets back here for the families in the town."

"Exactly," Ozil said. "That will enable us to quickly assist their removal." Ozil smiled broadly. "I am so proud of the way you and Rampart took the initiative to coordinate everything. A good head guardsman is proven by the way his men handle themselves without orders. Well done!"

"It wasn't me, Ozil," Saul said. "It was all Rampart."

"Someone coordinated Rampart's rescue," Ozil reminded while tapping Saul's chest, "and in doing so you and your fellow guardsmen probably did half our search for the willing already. I bet *they* find *us* as soon as we enter the town."

Saul laughed.

Dusk kicked up dirt with his hind legs and growled loudly. Both fae turned in his direction.

"Finally you remembered I'm here," Dusk said. "And let's not forget I jumped on this long before either of you. Why? Because my master was on the way to his death *after* uttering his dying wish for me to stay out of it. Well, I'm not sorry I disobeyed." The hound nudged Ozil's boot. "I was the one that *ordered* Saul to save Rampart. I was the one—"

"Hold on, hound!" Saul interrupted. "I never said I didn't appreciate your will to save Rampart. And I believe I solved your request quite efficiently." Saul scratched behind Dusk's left ear, and the hound's back foot scratched the air. "I didn't even mention that the others were already on it as soon as they heard of Rampart's capture. The guardsmen, along with your help, saved your master, and Rampart took it from there. Teamwork."

Dusk jerked his head from Saul's reach. The front half of his hairy body fell to the ground and his rump followed with a thump. "Listen, Saul, everything that happened after I swiftly rounded you up was destiny. Actually, all our fates started to take paths when the Erlking dragged Rampart out of his cell—the cell you were in, by the way." The animal raised his snout to Ozil and stretched his back legs out behind him on either side of a wagging tail. "I could tell Rampart knew I was still beside him. I was cloaked, for hell's sake, and still, the damned imp kept looking right at me as he dragged his shackled, bare feet across the castle floors, while the monster in the leather mask poked his back with a scepter. And not for a second did he show fear or pain."

"Of course not. He is a guardsman and that is our oath." Ozil chuckled.

"Show no fear. Be prepared. Anticipate the opposition," Saul said with a smile as Ozil joined in on the last sentence.

"Yeah, yeah," Dusk said, giving them the same amount of respect he'd received from the two fae earlier.

Dusk slowly rose to his feet and his nose bumped Ozil's chest armor. It left a large, green, snotty spot. "Look, when Rampart stumbled, I had a burning desire to get the demented arse-wipe's neck between my teeth.

"Listen, Ozil, Nereus spat out even more retaliations than Rampart's impending death because of Efrian's disloyalty and your escape. He was talking about publicly killing families in the hive just for the devil's entertainment. You really pushed his buttons, Ozil. That's when I almost uncloaked and Rampart shot me a 'warn them' look," the hellhound snorted at Saul, "and that's why everyone was ready when you got to the hive."

Ozil pulled a red scarf out of his boot and ran it vigorously over the slime on his chest plate. "Our destiny. Our fate, my arse. This is Coralina's destiny and the fate of her people. So, let's get on with it and worry less of who is responsible for Rampart's escape and the safety of my men's families." He shoved the scarf back into his boot and raised an arm to Saul. "Let's get moving. We have guardsmen to talk to, and a town to round up and evacuate."

Saul nodded. "I'm pleased to be beside you again, Captain."

"Well, I'm not!" Dusk said. "I'm going to Copper Groves to educate Rampart, now that *you* saved his arse."

Ozil turned to the hellhound. "Excellent! Have your master join us as soon as possible."

Dusk snorted. "I have a strong feeling about Nereus's next move. You want to hear it?"

"No," Ozil said. "We are wasting time, Hound."

"Too bad. I'm gonna tell you anyway because when I leave here it's what I'm gonna tell Ramp." The hound's maw turned up a grin. "I don't just think. I'm absolutely positive the idiot and his cohorts will heavily arm the castle from the inside with all the trustworthy guards they can find. I'll go even further and say he probably already has."

"Why would he have done that?" Ozil asked. "Escaping without notice would be almost impossible if we surround the castle."

"You want to explain how you obtained your reasoning and anything else you are keeping from us?" Saul asked.

"Not right now," Dusk said. "But I will be back to assist Ozil, and fetch you, Saul, after I talk to Rampart and Coralina. From what I'm thinking, Rampart may need you, so get Ozil squared away and be ready to head to Copper Groves."

"Don't you think you should inform us now?" Ozil gruffly said. "This isn't a one-dog show, fella. We all need to be on the same page."

"And I'm not leaving Ozil on a whim," Saul said.

Dusk closed his eyes. "I could tell you but what about the Nulls? Can they read minds? You willing to screw the pooch on this one if I tell you there's a—"

"—a damn good idea brewing, my man, and you're gonna keep it to yourself!" Ozil cut in and slapped his breastplate hard. "You tell them I said so, then get your hind-end back here with more information."

"I will, and by the time I come back, the Null will be no help." Dusk turned to trot away. "And I'm not your man, Ozil. I'm Rampart's hellion. You two get your job done and I'll do mine," the hellhound shouted as he broke into a sprint toward Copper Groves.

***

Famri took to the air and headed toward the hive followed by six guardsmen, all of which would be dead by midday. He had yet to select which of the six would be first accompanied by his family. His mood was aggravated by the fact he had murdered another five before leaving, piled them at the gates, and now could not trust the six guards that also merited death to bring the families back.

Famri's frustration turned to anger and it was all he could do to keep from screaming aloud when he found the hive empty. Not a soul, nor one of the king's drone wasps was to be seen. With great haste, he ordered the men to follow him back to town. When they arrived and realized the villagers had vacated, his mood moved from fuming to fear and tightened his groin.

Famri headed directly toward the guards' camp, and rage overwhelmed fear when he found no one there as well. *They must all be underground*, he thought, and ordered the six fae to search the tunnels and basements under the huts.

As soon as they left, Famri's legs buckled under him and he fell to his knees. He knew he should immediately go to the castle and inform the Erlking of these events but could not bring himself to move.

"Where have they gone? Who can hide a village of fae? Surely the Erlking hasn't lost his mind entirely? And he would no more kill them than move them all into the castle." Famri rubbed his temples. "I must be dreaming." His laughter bounced off the walls of the empty building. "Imagine, the guards in the castle and the townsfolk seeking safety with the Erlking. It's ludicrous!" He covered his face with his hands and laughed. "It's insane!" Famri said around manic giggles as he stood. "I must run to the castle to see if the mounds of dead are reaching the fortress's belfry!"

"Not so quickly," said a voice he knew well.

Famri's head shot toward the entrance. "Ozil! Have you won the war?" Famri babbled.

Ozil pulled his weapon. The sword blade glistened in a stream of light cast from a skylight overhead. He stepped slowly across the room and stood before Famri. "Your guardsmen seemed to have left you. Perhaps they are all hiding under a rock."

"You have no men at your back either, old man," Famri said. "Sheath your sword, you fool." He reached for his own weapon, and both fae realized Famri was carrying none.

Ozil tipped his blade to this boot and used his words carefully. "You have two choices. Let me lock you in the holding cell downstairs or die where you kneel."

***

Reka had left Rampart, Dusk, Coralina, Cal, and the jinn outside the tunnel where the guards' families and the townsfolk were hidden. She had asked for a reprieve as they began to discuss their plan for attack. Mabyn told Reka she would go before the others could answer and explained she would check on them. The rest of the group asked no questions but decided to stay close to the entrance until Reka's return.

Reka spread her wings and took to the air. She did not drop them until after she flew through an open window in the guardsmen's quarters and down the cellar stairs and stood before Famri.

"I won't take the time to talk to you, especially since Ozil explained you have no information or a call for our cause. You were a vile changeling and only became worse with age. I'm going to kill you, Famri. But at least your head won't be on one of the Erlking's poles."

Reka called the magic burbling in the bottom of her stomach, up through her esophagus and nasal passages into the area behind her eyes.

Famri watched the queen's eyes turn into blue flames. "Please. Don't do this, Queen Reka. I will do anything you say," he pleaded.

"No. You won't," Reka said. "And I am no queen. Nereus often spoke of you when he visited me in the hive. He also watched you grow into your sickness and often told me that if he ever had a son, he wished it would be like you. Did you know Mabyn refused him the gift of a male heir?"

Famri shook his head and stood. He placed his hands on the iron bars in front of him. He had no time to entertain the compliment Reka just afforded him. The blood in his body began to seep, like sweat, from the pores on his skin. His eyes were wide as they darted over his hands and arms. He swiped his brow, and blood dripped onto his boots and the cell floor.

"I will end your life with a great deal of pain," Reka said. "But swiftly, although you are not worthy of it. It's a shame you have no powers. Your strength is in your hatred. And that won't save you now."

Reka's eyes closed and her lips parted. A stream of fire shot from her mouth and muscled its way into every orifice on Famri's face. He had no time to scream. His head exploded into a thousand little bits of bone, brain, blood, hair, and flesh.

***

"Anyway," Saul said, "it runs directly under the castle."

Coralina, Rampart, Cal, Aldul, and Dusk huddled around the campfire just inside Copper Grove's underground tunnel.

"I remember that place," Coralina said. "My mother took me through the caves to meet Nereus. He wanted nothing of me so I began to explore a small pond down there. When my mother warned me not to get into the water, Nereus snickered and told my mother to let me be. I immediately disliked him and was pleased when he escorted my mother through a door and disappeared."

"I bet you played in the pool," Cal said and smiled.

Coralina teased him with a frown. "No. I was very obedient back then."

"Why do I doubt that?" Rampart asked Cal.

Coralina laughed. "The two of you bring out the worst and the best in me."

Smoke from the fire mingled with the colorful smoke of Aldul's body shape and made him look like a wavering rainbow.

Mabyn walked out of the cave and sat beside Abdul. Reka is pleasantly handing out rations to the fae, now. I think her flight soothed her.

Rampart laughed. "If Reka was headed where I think she was headed, Famri is a pool of bubbling blood with bits and pieces of his fae flesh floating in it by now. And that is what has soothed her."

"Well, only if Reka took pity on him," Mabyn added with a chuckle.

Coralina laughed. "Let's hope not."

"I'd hate to see the dungeon walls if she didn't," Dusk said, and laid a big black paw on Rampart's folded knee.

"So, what's the plan?" Aldul asked of Rampart and Saul.

Rampart said, "Half of us will hit the tunnels that lead into the castle through the dungeons."

"That leaves the rest of us to take position at the front gates," Coralina said.

"Hey," Dusk said, "why does everyone undermine, and in this case, totally ignore my capabilities, never mind my orchestration in all of this?"

"I saved the best for last," Rampart said. "Without you, how would we communicate? Head back to fill Ozil in."

***

Ozil and Dusk stood alone as the many moons in Faery Lands became soft white circles on a deepening blue sphere above them. They paused within the woods where they had a clear view of the castle gates before them and the town to their right.

"Be right back," Dusk said, and disappeared under a cloak of cover.

***

Coralina, Cal, Mabyn, and Aldul crouched behind a gathering of shrubs beside the castle on the right side of the gates, all eyes on the forest behind the town.

"I don't see them," Coralina said.

"And darkness will soon be on us," Mabyn added.

"Coralina." Although Aldul's voice was soft, its tone demanded attention. "Are you sure we can trust the hellhound to deliver proper directions?"

"While that mutt has been nothing but a thorn in the left side of my ass, he is loyal to his master," Coralina whispered. "And I am very sure—"

"Hold on," Cal hushed the fae, and pointed toward the woods off to the right, "Watch," he said, and pointed to an area of woods to the left of them closer to the town.

Mabyn giggled. Everyone turned toward her. She turned her lips under her teeth and held them there for a heartbeat then pooched them like a fish. It was clear she was trying to hold back a laugh. "That light is Ozil's armor catching what is left of the day. Never thought I'd be happy he is so obsessed with its shine."

"Crap," a voice said from behind, and all four jumped to attention.

"I wanted to point that out," Dusk said, and dropped his cloak of cover.

CHAPTER TWENTY-TWO

Ash in the Water

"Damn it, Dusk!" Coralina shoved her palm against the hell hound's chest. "Don't sneak up on us, especially behind enemy lines. We could have killed you."

"Uh huh, sure," Dusk sat with a smirk. "Not going to happen. You fae have such amusing looks when you're startled." He rolled on his back and wiggled his butt and head in different directions.

Cal grunted and turned back toward the castle walls. "I've never really cared for hell hounds," he said. "Can't say this one is changing my opinion."

Dusk stretched and poked the angel's back with his paw. "Come on, I heard you were supposed to have a sense of humor. Don't go all pompous angel on me."

With irritation, Coralina reached out and grabbed a handful of the hound's chin hair and twisted his head to catch her stern gaze. "Dusk, please tell me you're here to report something," she said in a throaty whisper. "Because I swear, if you keep this up and attract attention for no good reason, I'll...."

Dusk wormed his head from her grasp. "What? Kick my ass?' He nodded toward where they saw Ozil. "I came here to let you know everything is set. Ozil is waiting for the last bit of sunlight to drain from the sky before he starts the attack. He and Rampart, accompanied by half breeds, are going to approach from different angles to make as much of a ruckus as possible. It should give you guys enough of a distraction to sneak into the castle and do what you got to do."

A thin smile spread on Coralina's face, but soon faded. The information was given so casually, as if they were planning a surprise party. But the gravity of the moment weighed on her. This was their chance. More likely than not, their only one. If the Erlking survived the night, everything they'd worked and suffered for would perish under his wrath. "That's great news," she said as upbeat as she could. "As soon as he makes his move, Cal will take us into the Gray and get us behind the castle walls."

Aldul's smoky eyes turned toward her. "My people will meet us inside. If enough of the guard move to deal with Ozil's distraction, we should be able to carve out a path to the throne room."

"Should," Coralina murmured. "That's the word that's bothering me."

Aldul shrugged. "There is no guarantee what we'll find once we're inside. Nereus has been fortifying his castle since Rampart's failed execution. And he's been suspicious of the jinn since the last... discussion I had with him. The point is we won't know what we're dealing with till we get in there."

"I know. I know," Coralina said. "I just hate playing it by ear." She leaned her back against the rock and dug her toes into the cool soil. "And I hope the fae we brought are ready to use the skills Cal has helped them with. If they can just fend off anything outside the castle and help the townsfolk left behind, that will be enough.

Mabyn laughed. "If it makes you feel any better, I can guarantee Nereus isn't making the best decisions. I know my husband, and when he feels cornered, he acts on emotions. Usually ruthless and merciless emotions, granted, but clear-headed strategy goes out the window."

Cal shook his head. "You know what, that doesn't make me feel any better. We are about to charge headfirst into that ruthless cornered animal," he said. "He doesn't need a masterplan when we're arriving at his door, and I don't like the idea of him getting imaginative with how he's going to..."

Before he could finish his thought, a whooshing sound came from where they had seen Ozil. The group turned to see a giant fireball light a trail through the dark sky. It sailed almost majestically through the still air till it collided with the castle wall with a loud thud. The wall seemed unharmed, but the fire dripped down the stone like liquid before pooling on the ground.

Coralina smiled as more fiery orbs launched toward the castle. The display was dramatic, impressively intimidating and impossible to ignore. Exactly what she wanted in a distraction. "Alright, that's our cue," she said, pulling herself into a crouching position. "The Guard should be moving to defensive positions soon."

Armored heads brandishing torches began popping up around the spires, and the clanging of troop movement rattled the stone walls.

"Damn him to Hell," Cal popped his head up. "Sounds like Nereus has a whole army in there."

Aldul nodded. "There's no way we'd survive a full-on assault, that's for sure," he said. "But fortunately for us we don't have to. We just need to sneak by the entrance. Once we're in the winding corridors, they won't be able to pursue us easily." Colorful strings of smoke wafted toward the castle. "I must meet my people and give the order to breach through the arrowslits. I'll see you soon, my friends." His smokey form whisked upward, disappearing into the night.

Coralina nodded at Cal. "Alright, I guess it's really time to do this."

The Watcher nodded back, sliced his hand through the air, and cut a passage through reality. Pulling the sides like a curtain, he exposed the space between worlds called The Gray. Coralina, Mabyn, and Dusk hurried into the colorless space as he closed the curtain behind.

They ran for the castle and passed through its walls like the stone was nothing but air. Once inside, they saw heavily armored guards, swords drawn and wielding shields. The main doors soon fell open, and the horde ran out, ready to meet the resistance. Their bodies rushed past the group. Even safe in the Gray, Coralina found herself bracing for impact as they passed through her. She closed her eyes against the onslaught of screaming, and snarling faces. After the commotion past, she opened them and watched the bridge retract, but she caught a brief glimpse of the half fae charging toward the guard, their newfound magic swirling toward those who would try to oppress it. Her chest tightened, and her eyes glazed over with mixed feelings of respect and fear for their wellbeing.

Cal reached out and took Coralina by the hand. "Come on," he said, pulling her deeper into the castle. "We can't stay here. They're focused on what's going on outside, but some fae are strong enough to detect us even in the Gray. We'll be safer once we're further inside."

The group continued past the hall and up the stairs. Guardsmen clambered past oblivious to their presence, and with arms full, ran munitions to other posts. Once the hallways thinned and no guards were present, Cal once again opened the Gray and exposed the world of color. "Alright," he whispered. "Everyone out."

Coralina and Mabyn brushed past him, but Dusk lingered. "Wait, this is stupid," Dusk snarled. "Why aren't we taking this all the way to the throne room?"

"Because I'm freaked out by the Null devices Coralina told me about," Cal said. "I have no idea how that'll react with my magic, and I don't want to get all the way to Nereus just to find we can't leave the Gray."

Dusk snorted but complied.

As they continued down the hallway, the sounds of battle vibrated through the stonework. Explosions rattled the candlesticks in their holders, and wind gusts from air fae whistled past the windows. For a moment, Coralina regretted leaving the half fae to battle without her, wishing to fight alongside those she'd helped train. But she knew she was where she needed to be. The most important thing tonight was bringing the Erlking to justice. Even taking the castle would mean nothing if he slipped away into the night. As long as he lived, his followers would still fear to turn from him. And the land would have no peace.

"Stop right there!" a voice came from behind them. Coralina turned to see a group of ten Guardsmen, swords drawn.

"Didn't get very far, did we?!" Dusk spat at Cal as he ran down the hallway, long claws tapping against the stone floor.

Cal didn't respond but followed the hellhound around the corner. At the end of the next corridor more guardsmen poured in, teeth bared and anger flaring in their eyes.

"Shit," Cal murmured while conjuring his sword of light. "We can't take a whole castle of them."

Coralina braced and prepared to strike at them. But before she could, green and gold smoke burst from the wall. Aldul slammed the guard closest to Cal with an eruption of dark energy that knocked him back and into the other men.

"Jinn!" a voice rang out. The guard halted their approach, the anger in their eyes turned to fear.

Aldul had a look of amusement on the hazy features of his face. "Oh, I'm afraid it's even worse than you think."

On cue, other jinn swarmed down the corridor, their smokey bodies blocking light with swirls of red, blue, orange, and purple smoke. It wafted around the guards, hitting them with spells from all sides.

"This way," Mabyn said, kicking open a door. Coralina, Cal, and Dusk followed her into the main dining hall. One unlucky guard tried to follow, but a jinn opened the ground beneath him and sealed him in a cold, rock grave.

"We'll halt them here," Aldul called after them. "Get to the throne room."

"Don't have to tell me twice," Dusk shouted back as paws slipped on well-polished stone to gain traction.

They followed Mabyn through the back of the hall and into another corridor, moving quickly to get away from the commotion behind them. "This is an alternate way to get to the throne," Mabyn said. "But I was hoping not to come this way."

"Yeah?" Coralina asked. "And why is that?"

"Because the only way through is to pass by the armory," Mabyn replied. "There are always guards there, protecting the armaments from their enemies. And a good number of them, too."

"Swell," Dusk laughed. "The armory, so they'll have all the really good weapons with them."

Mabyn nodded. "Yes, but I think I can get us past them," she said.

Before Coralina could ask how, Mabyn stopped at a junction of the hallway. She held her index finger against her lips before peeking around the corner. Coralina followed her lead and cautiously peered down the corridor. At the end of it, a large wood door stood open, a dozen guards rifled through rows of shelves within, filled to bursting with swords, maces, and various other weapons.

Mabyn reached her hand out and slowly wiggled her fingers, as if she were plucking invisible strings in the air. Her hand waved serenely through the air like a conductor before an orchestra. Slowly, the guards slowed their sorting. Their eyes glazed as they looked around, as if they were seeing for the first time. They hung their arms at their sides and began wandering around carelessly.

"Umm... Mabyn?" Cal whispered. "What exactly are you doing to them?"

Mabyn smiled. "It's alright. You can talk normally," she said, standing up. "They won't bother us now." She began walking toward the guards. They noticed her but showed no alarm. "That's one of my powers, to control emotions and actions like one feels in a drug induced state." She walked up to the nearest guard and patted his shoulder. "These guys are more relaxed right now than they ever have been in their lives." She turned to Cal. "And they won't remember a thing."

"What else can you do?" Dusk asked.

"If you keep doubting our abilities," Mabyn said with a grin, "I may show you."

"I can do a stint of as high as a star in a dark faery sky, but I'd like to be able to look back on if fondly."

"You are a piece of work," Coralina said. "I'm glad you are Rampart's problem and not mine."

"You see Rampart?" Dusk looked around. "I don't."

"Ugh! Do you always have to have the last word?"

"Not today," Dusk said.

A tall guard near the door leaned his back against the wall and slowly slid down till he sat cross legged on the floor. His eyes stuck in a thousand-yard stare. Coralina bent down and waved her hand in front of his face. If he noticed, he gave no indication.

"Okay, that's pretty cool," Coralina said. "Why didn't you do that earlier?"

"It doesn't work on anybody with already heightened emotions," she said. "The other guards had too much adrenaline pumping to have this kind of effect."

Coralina smiled thinking of what a fool Nereus was for not accepting Mabyn into the guard. She would be very useful helping soldiers control their emotions on the battlefield. "Okay, that works," Coralina said. "Let's just let them trip down paradise lane and be on our way." She moved down the hall a few feet before she realized Mabyn hadn't moved. She turned to see the queen's smile.

"Actually," Mabyn said, "I think I'll stay here." She waved her hand again and the guards perked up. They drew their swords and encircled her. A couple of them murmured about having to protect the queen.

"Mabyn?" Coralina said. "What are you doing?"

"There's not much I can help you with against Nereus," she said. "He's nothing but a ball of rage, immune to my manipulation. But here, I can use these men to keep a main source of armaments away from the rest of the army, another line of protection in case any of them get past the jinn."

Coralina shook her head. "No way I'm leaving you here alone. It's too dangerous."

Dusk walked in front of Mabyn and sat down. "I'll stay with her," he said. "Rampart's still out on the battlefield. If I can stop the guard from getting these weapons, then at least in a small way I can feel I'm keeping my...only friend safe."

Coralina and Cal exchanged looks. Without a word, both knew what the other was thinking.

Can the two of us take the Erlking alone?

Coralina didn't know, but she saw the point Mabyn was making. And if her powers wouldn't work on Nereus, it would make more sense for her to hang back. Not only for her own safety, but as a failsafe. If Coralina were to fall in the battle, Mabyn would be the next natural leader for the rebels. Rampart and Ozil trusted her knowledge and judgment, and she would carry on if the worst happened tonight.

"Oh, stop looking like you doubt yourselves," Dusk said. "You two have a gift. A personal reason to do the job. Go for it."

Coralina smiled at the hellhound and nodded to Mabyn before grabbing Cal's arm and pulling him down the hallway.

"The throne room is down the corridor and to the left," Mabyn shouted after them, her voice shrouded by the sound of their footsteps on the stone floor.

The two of them followed the hall till it opened into a bigger corridor, this one heavily decorated with blue and silver flags draping tall pillars. A crimson carpet led to two large heavy wooden doors.

"Well, this just reeks of Nereus's ego, doesn't it?" Cal asked. "I guess we found the throne room."

Coralina glanced around. "Strange, I thought there would be a battalion of guards to sneak past. Where is everyone?"

"Maybe they're all out dealing with your army and the jinn?" Cal said.

"Or maybe they're all lying in wait," Coralina said. "Keep your eyes open just in case." Her mind drifted to the possibility they weren't there because Nereus had already escaped, but she didn't want to say that out loud.

They walked cautiously through the abandoned entrance. Its emptiness gave Coralina the creeps. The only sound was the muffled sounds of the battle outside resonating through the wall. Her eyes kept jutting toward dark corners, expecting the enemy to jump out at them. But nothing did. It should have been a relief to Coralina, but it weighed her with a sense of foreboding. *Nereus would never leave himself open like this*, she thought, *at least not without a plan.*

As they approached the throne doors, a rumble bubbled from beneath the castle. A deafening boom cut through the silent room as the whole castle seemed to shift on its foundation. Coralina and Cal grabbed each other as dusty debris shook free from the tall ceiling. The flags on the pillars shook from their perches and floated to the ground. Then, just as quickly as it started, it dissipated. Leaving only the crumbling sound of ceiling fragments as a reminder.

"What the hell are they doing out there?" Cal asked.

Coralina frowned. "I don't think that was from our people. The rebels don't have explosives that could hit the castle that hard."

"What about the half fae?" Cal asked. "They've gotten powerful, especially when they get emotional. And I bet they're pretty angry right now."

Coralina brushed dust off the top of her blonde hair. "There's no way they'd hit the castle with anything that powerful while we are inside." She waited to see if the rumbling would start again, but nothing happened. "I don't know what that was, but we don't have time to waste thinking about it. Let's finish this."

They turned toward the large doors separating them from the throne room, only an arm's length away. Cal chuckled. "Man. I can't believe not too long ago my main concern was trying to choke down cafeteria food at high school in the human world. Now I'm charging into a castle in Faery Lands, trying to dethrone a tyrant king." He shook his head. "You know, when I found you in Perdition, drinking at that broken down bar, you were settled in and ready to spend the rest of your life there. So much so you literally fought me so you could stay."

Cal glanced at her out of the side of his vision. "Do you ever wish you never left? That you could have that quiet life back where you don't have to worry about anyone other than yourself?"

Coralina's focus remained forward, her expression unmoving. "No," she said. "No, I do not." She forcefully planted the palm of her hands against the wooden doors and pushed with enough force they flung open and slammed against the walls. She stormed in with Cal in tow as if she expected the whole army to be waiting on the other side. Though, once again, they were met with no resistance. No guards, magic, or traps sprung to stop them. At the end of the crimson carpet sat an empty throne, flanked by the Erlking's twin advisors, each with a Null hovering around their silver hair.

Coralina's eyes narrowed. Her rage boiled as her eyes landed on the empty throne. "Where is my father?" she growled as she stomped toward the two advisors. "If you think a Null will keep you safe from me..."

Thallia raised her hand with her palm toward them. "My brother and I have no intention of fighting. Our way has never been one of brute strength, but of logic and reason."

"Logic?! Reason?!" Coralina barked. "No one who willingly serves under a madman while he commits genocide can dare claim they have those traits."

Thallia lowered her hand and clasped them in front of her. "Perhaps so," she said calmly. "But such things are not for us to question."

Coralina stopped at the base of the stairs leading to the throne and spat on the carpet. "Enough of your pompous bullshit. I asked you a question. Tell me where the Erlking is."

Diaspor opened his arms. "Of course. That is why we're here."

Cal frowned. "You mean, you guys are turning on Nereus, too?"

"No," Diaspor's voice deepened. "Our loyalty is, as it always has been, to the throne." He mimicked his sister's movement and clasped his hands in front of himself. "Erlking Nereus has instructed us to wait here to deliver a message in case of his daughter's arrival."

Coralina's eyes narrowed. "What message?"

"He wanted us to tell you that he won't be chased from his castle," Diaspor said. "That he wouldn't allow the unworthy to sit on his throne and let filth spread across his lands." His voice softened when he met Coralina's fiery gaze. "Those are his words, of course. Not ours. He awaits you underneath the castle at the Lake of Life."

Cal scoffed and turned to Coralina. "That's the lake you were telling me about, the one that connects to the water table for the entire forest?" he asked. "I couldn't come up with a worse place to fight one of the most powerful water fae alive."

Thallia stepped forward. "I believe that is the point," she said. "The Erlking enjoys grand shows of power and will only fight in an area he knows he has the advantage. Nevertheless, that is where he waits."

Coralina licked her lips. "Nereus has had the advantage since the beginning, and now we're standing in his throne room, our weapons beating his castle walls. We've beaten the odds before, and with the mood I'm in, he'll need more than a little water to protect himself from me." She stepped closer to Thallia till she was in arms reach of her. "How do we reach the Lake of Life from here?"

"We can lead you to the entrance, but the Erlking gave orders we weren't supposed to enter the cavern," Thallia said. "At that point, you'll be on your own."

"And what about that earthquake we felt a minute ago?" Cal asked. "It felt like it came from under the castle. Was that Nereus's doing?"

Diaspor shrugged. "If it was, we weren't made aware of its happening beforehand," he said, bowing his head. "It seems our council is being needed for less and less these days."

"We serve the throne," Thallia snapped at her brother. "It doesn't serve us."

"And what if someone else were to sit upon that throne?" Cal asked, stepping closer to Coralina. "Like a certain pissed off rebel leader?"

The twins exchanged glances, searching for a diplomatic response. "We were loyal advisors to Nereus's father, just as we have been to him," Thallia said, putting thought into each of her words. "And if his time were to come to pass, his daughter as well."

Coralina's jaw clenched at the reminder of being Nereus's daughter. "Well, I suppose that's something," she said. "But for now all I need from you two to take me where dear old dad is."

***

Coralina and Cal traveled down the winding tunnel. The air grew cold and heavy with moisture from the lake below. The cave floor was slick with a thin layer of water. Coralina had to catch herself several times to keep from tumbling down into the dark chasm. The tremor they felt before erupted again, bellowing from below and shaking loose stone from the cave ceiling. The twins had no answer on the cause, but there was one thing Coralina knew. Somehow, someway, Nereus was responsible.

As the cave leveled out, the tunnel opened into a massive cavern. Bioluminescent lights splotched the ceiling and walls with a soft green glow. Underneath, the lake of life bubbled and churned, but even though it boiled, it gave no heat. Waves slammed against the cavern's sides sending water and a deafening roar climbing up the cavern walls.

In the middle of the turbulent lake hovered Nereus. His dark form loomed with outstretched arms, bobbing up and down above the waves.

"Well," Cal shouted above the water's roar, "we were right. He's definitely up to something."

The cavern shook as the water rose. Geysers sprung around the lake high enough to lick the ceiling.

"Seems that way," Coralina said. "Let's go find out what it is. Time to put on your game face."

Cal smiled. His wings materialized behind him, his angelic wing in radiant light, and his jinn gift out of swirling green and gold smoke. As the fae energies came to the surface, his skin turned ashen and cracked like embers and veins glowed red like lava. Orange flames burst from his hair, dancing upward in smokeless light. "Alright," he said. "I'm good to go."

The two flew above the turbulent waters. The spray misted the air with cool moisture. Nereus floated in place as he watched their approach but did nothing. He smiled as they neared, as if they were old friends coming to greet him. It made Coralina's skin crawl.

"I had hoped you wouldn't make it this far, my daughter," Nereus said, his voice smooth and calming. "But I see once again, you defy the odds."

Coralina sneered. "Despite your guards' best efforts."

"Yes, their best efforts." He sighed. "That, unfortunately, may be true. In all honesty, when your rebellion first started, it was barely spoken of in my presence. I had trusted those under me to enact my will swiftly and efficiently. It was thought your efforts would be crushed within a few weeks." Nereus shook his head. "And yet, here we are. To think it would come to this."

The waters rose again. Its shifting splintered the ceiling. Boulders rained down and splashed in the lake around them.

"What are you doing, Nereus?" Cal yelled at the king.

Nereus's smile disappeared as he turned to the angel. "Ah, you brought the motherless one with you I see, and he's contaminated himself even further with jinn filth."

The fire in Cal's veins burned brighter, but he said nothing.

"No matter. I'll answer your abomination's question." Nereus faced back to Coralina. "Your rebellion has showed me any Erlking's greatest fear. Not the threat of spears or magic, but of a dark contaminant that has spread through the heart of its people. It is the Erlking's right to rule the people, and for them to serve his will without question. Had one or two villages succumbed to your poisonous words, I could have written off the betrayal as a few weak-willed fae losing their way. A matter that could be dealt with swiftly without further harm." Nereus's expression darkened as his eyes bored into Coralina. "But your infection has spread further than even I could have anticipated. My people disobey simple instruction, my guard turned on me and failed to do my will, even attacking me in broad daylight for all to see. In times like these, there is but one option, to cleanse the land."

The lake burst underneath them, in a wave of cold water.

Nereus closed his eyes. "It's almost ready. Soon, I will have gathered enough pressure within the lake of life, it will rise to the surface; a tsunami with enough force to obliterate the castle and surrounding city. The flash flood will radiate into the forest, wiping it clean from the disease you've inflicted upon it." The light from under his leather mask shined bright and created beams that jutted out into the dark cave, but Nereus showed no notice of the pain. "Within minutes, the forest will be underwater, along with the fae civilization."

Coralina floated backward, as if she were struck in the chest. She thought she knew the depravity of the king, but even in her dark recesses of her mind, Coralina didn't think him capable of such an act. "You... you'd kill everyone?" She gasped. "Even those still loyal to you, the ones out there risking their lives for your rule."

"If they had stopped you from reaching me, then no, I would not," Nereus snarled. "But everyone above has either betrayed me or failed me. And I have no need for either traitors or failures in my kingdom."

Cal drifted closer to Coralina. "If you do this, you'll doom your race," he said. "There aren't enough fae outside the lands to keep your civilization alive. Soon, all your people, your culture, it'll just fade away."

"Let it!" Nereus shouted as the water beneath him began to swirl. "The fae are nothing without their king. If my rule is to end, so should its people." He reached up and tore the leather mask from his face and threw it into the water, releveling the bright burning handprint beneath. The glamour he held to shroud his true appearance melted away. The smooth creamy skin thinned and grayed, it tightened on his bones till he resembled more of an undead creature than a fae. His delicate wings cracked and decayed, leaving tattered webbing on skeletal wings. "I am the fae!" he bellowed, his blue eyes glowing brightly in their dark sockets. "They began with me, and they end with me!"

Coralina dove forward in effort to catch Nereus off guard. Her fist swung but caught nothing but air as he swung his body midair. The spinning water underneath rose up in a tornado of water rotating toward the Erlking. Coralina barely had time to jut out of the way before it encircled him. The column of water continued upward till it hit the cavern ceiling. The spinning water ground away at the rock, sending debris raining down around it. Nereus's figure was only visible as a shadow behind the water, his skeletal arms outstretched directing the waterspout.

Coralina lashed out, sending razor thin bursts of air toward the spout. They sent splashes of water into the air, but barely scratched the surface. In an effort to slow the spout's rotation, she focused and began spinning the air around it in the opposite direction, but as she focused, tentacle like streams of water sprouted from the lake below and lashed like whips toward her. Breaking her concentration as they tore clothes and flesh.

In the distance, she could see Cal charge full speed at the cyclone. He pushed through the outer layer, but before he was in reach of the king the water's rotation overpowered him. He spun upward till he was thrown from the spout backward into a large chunk of falling debris.

Coralina flew quickly to Cal as he steadied himself. "Are you okay?" she asked.

The dazed angel took a moment before answering. "Yeah, I'm fine, just got the wind knocked out of me. I told you this was the worst place to fight him."

The two watched as Nereus glided toward them. More tendrils of water rose from the lake, slithering toward them like snakes.

Coralina guided them backward to create distance from them and the approaching threats. Her mind raced, with enough effort she believed she could counter the spout's rotation, but even with Cal distracting him, as soon as Nereus felt the air moving, he'd switch focus. She needed something instant, some way to lower his barrier and give them a chance to reach him.

A thought entered her mind. It was a technique she'd never tried before, and one she didn't know would work on such a large scale. But her powers, like most fae, became more powerful when emotions spiked, and she was certainly very emotional right now. "Cal, do you think you can distract him for a bit?"

"Heh." Cal chuckled. "I guess we can find out. But whatever you're going to do, try to be quick. He's too smart to take his attention off you for too long."

She nodded, and he flew into the gauntlet of lashing water, spinning and dodging as he went. He neared the cyclone of water surrounding Nereus and sent streams of red flames into its side. The water hissed and steamed but was replaced quicker than Cal could evaporate it.

That's fine, Coralina thought. *Just keep him busy.*

She reached out her hand and focused on the air in the cavern. She felt it swirling around the cyclone, as turbulent as the water below. Her eyes closed as she attuned with it, every gust and disturbance in the air she could feel, as if the air around was an extension of her own body. Then she pushed deeper, till she could feel the air trapped in the water spinning around Nereus, every bubble caught in the raging cyclone. She continued to delve as deep as her mind would allow, till she could feel deep into the molecular level. It was a feeling she had never felt before, a complete oneness with the environment around her. It was as if every molecule of oxygen was in the palm of her hand.

Coralina opened her eyes. Beads of sweat dripped from her eyelashes. She could feel the great strain of what she was doing upon her body, and yet, she couldn't help but smile through the pain. "Hey, Nereus!" she called out through the great cave.

The Erlking's shadowy figure turned toward her.

"Do you know what water is without oxygen?" Coralina's canines slipped under her smile. "Nothing, just like you."

With her last bit of strength, she yanked as hard as possible on every bubble, pocket, and molecule of oxygen in the waterspout. It bowed and flexed under the pressure, till the air exploded out with enough force to disintegrate the water tendrils surrounding it. The booming sound was louder than any explosion Coralina had ever heard and the column of water protecting Nereus vaporized into nothing more than swirling steam and gas.

Coralina could see Nereus's face twist in rage. "You insolent brat!" he shouted. "You have no idea what horror I'll inflict upon you! You'll beg for the quick death I was about to bestow upon you once..."

His tantrum was interrupted by Cal swooping in and tackling him midair. Before Nereus could react, Cal brought his palm lit with holy fire down on the unmarked side of his face. Nereus's scream echoed through the cavern as the fire burned him down to the bone. He tried to twist and squirm out of his grasp, but Cal pinned the withered king to his body. In desperation, Nereus pulled a dagger from his belt and quickly stabbed it into the angel's side.

Cal cried out in pain and released his grip on the Erlking and swirled backward to avoid another strike from Nereus's blade. His wings fluttered erratically as he held his side, gold blood seeping through his fingers. Coralina flew to him as quickly as her tired wings would let her.

"Oh my God," she said, wrapping her arms around him for support. "How bad is it? Let me see."

Cal grunted. "It's fine. Really," he said through pained breaths. "I've been through worse. The dagger missed anything important in there. Just hurts like hell."

Coralina let out a sigh of relief. But the respite didn't last long. "I'm glad you're okay, but I don't know for how long." Her gaze drifted toward Nereus writhing in pain. "I'm tapped out. Seriously, I'm surprised I'm still flying. And now with your wound, I don't know how we're going to take him down."

To her surprise, Cal smirked. "Yeah, well, I'm guessing he'll do a pretty good job of that himself," he said. "But we're going to have to wait and see."

Coralina gave him a quizzical look.

Cal pointed to Nereus and said nothing.

Nereus flailed in the air, screaming obscenities into the dark. He wrenched his hand away from his face long enough to see the new glowing handprint shinning even brighter than the first.

"How dare you lay your hand on me," Nereus screamed. "You're filth, you're disease! You think just because you have angel blood within you that gives you the right to touch someone like me? I am holy. I am the divine," he spat. "Someone as impure as yourself doesn't deserve to be in my presence. I'll eradicate you. You and all those like you!" The whole flame rooted into his cheeks, spread, encompassing his whole face. "I'll find your family, your friends. Tear down the gates of heaven themselves if I must. Your father will suffer the same end I inflicted upon your mother. I'll leave you an orphan weeping over your family's grave."

The fire spread through the rest of his head and down his shoulders. The pain must have been extraordinary, but it did nothing more than fuel rage. "All my enemies will crumble to my feet. The jinn will meet the end they should have so many years ago. Earth, Heaven, Hell, they'll all learn their place, bowing to me. I'm superior to all. Any who say otherwise I'll have their flesh flayed from their bones and presented to their families." The fire spread through his legs, and chunks of ashy flesh flaked from his bones and drifted into the lake below. Nereus giggled. "Yes; when I'm done, no one but the worthy will remain. You'll see. It'll be a paradise. A paradise!" His giggles erupted into mad laughter. It continued till the laughter was but an echo from the drifting ash that was once Nereus, Erlking of the fae.

As the last flake fell, the waters below rested. The bubbling subsided and the crashing waves smoothed into stillness. The cave became peaceful, even beautiful.

Coralina and Cal's strength gave out. They fell into the calm lake and floated on their backs. Cal's fae form faded away. "All the way to the end. He still could have saved himself," he said. "All he had to do was let go of the anger and hate within him."

Coralina thought of several remarks she could have made. But none seemed worthy of the situation. Nereus was dead, his terror was quelled, and everything she and her rebels had fought so hard to accomplish had finally been achieved. There were no words worthy of this moment. Somehow, the only appropriate sound was the silence of the cave, and the trickling of the water as it receded back into rivers that would heal the land.

CHAPTER TWENTY-THREE

The Beginning

The sun struggled over the turrets and cast light over the darkness of yesterday. Its almighty elegance beamed a slow but steady path across the grass as Coralina landed in front of the castle and took in the castle grounds. Her breath caught in her throat as the sun found its way into Nereus's dark garden; the horrific flora of silhouettes tainted its beauty. Her heart tightened; her breath caught in her throat. She tried to move but her legs were weak. She raised her hand to wipe a tear from her cheek when a rainbow of sparkles followed a shaded silhouette across the grass in front of the skeletal remains.

Coralina blinked her eyes and followed the sparkles upward. Calastair, the watcher that had been a big part of her life over the last couple of years, flew by. And, as always, here he was again when she needed him most. The angel's feathered wing fluttered in the sunlight igniting its red tips, and Calastair's other wing, the one Abdul had gifted him, sprinkled another path of color. As the sparkles fell over the bones of her brethren impaled in the Erlking's horrid garden, the skeletal figures fell like sand in an hourglass.

A soft breeze lifted the particles before they fell into the blades of grass around Coralina's bare feet. It carried the remains of fae that had died for this day along the rays of sunlight. She turned, reached up, and felt them brush goosebumps on her arms. She watched the wind lift the remnants higher. They sparkled like morning dew in the rays of sunlight before disappearing over the streets of the now bustling town before her.

Coralina spread her wings to catch the warmth of the sunlight and smiled up at Calastair. He waved a farewell and disappeared into the brightness of the sun above her. She knew he had entered The Gray.

Rampart's deep voice caught her attention from across the courtyard. His eyes caught hers and he took flight from the guards' quarters. She rose to join him.

"Ozil just informed me the blackness is receding back into the Bad Lands and the rivers are running through the countryside." A smile spread across Rampart's face.

Coralina pushed a clump of wispy white hair over her shoulder, and it danced in the air along her back. "I bet the caverns and caves are filling up, too."

Seconds later, they landed at the guards' quarters. "Have you chosen your head guardsmen team?" Rampart asked.

"I have," Coralina said, "and about to announce—"

"Will it be Ozil?" Rampart pushed Coralina's words aside with a smile lighting hopeful eyes.

"Yes, indeed, with Mabyn at his side." Coralina ignored the disappointment in Rampart's eyes. She hurriedly entered the building full of fae guards she knew Rampart thought he would be managing after today.

***

Coralina stood on the scaffolding Nereus had installed in the map room of the castle. A wearisomeness fell over her as she watched the townsfolk making their way to her coronation. She didn't turn when she heard the heavy wooden door open. She knew it was Rampart.

The deep throaty bong from the belfry officially announcing the death of an Erlking sounded louder today, and it would continue to ring until Coralina's coronation. She should be below, dressed in her cloak, and ready for Rampart to escort her to the throne room, but there was something else to address, and it was as important as the crown she would soon be wearing.

Rampart climbed the scaffolding and joined her.

A question hung in Coralina's mouth, and she swallowed hard.

"You look like a Queen, My Lady," Rampart said, hands joined behind his back. "Shall we?" he asked, and swung an arm toward the map room door.

Coralina forced a smile. "But I'm not ready."

"No buts," Rampart said, and placed a hand on the small of her back to guide her off the scaffolding.

"I need to remove this awful platform," Coralina mumbled softly while trying to gather words she'd tossed around for days and was now stepping all over them. Coralina knew she was at the fork of a road that Rampart was about to lead her down.

"...uh huh," Rampart was saying, "so, you can handle the scaffolding tomorrow. Today you take your rightful place on the throne."

It's now or never, she told herself as they both stepped off the steps of the scaffolding. Coralina turned her back on Rampart and moved to a chair in front of a table with the map of her kingdom laid out in front of her. "I want to talk to you first."

"We will talk later." Rampart brushed by on his way to the exit. "It's time I went down to the throne room with the others."

"I don't know if I'm—"

Rampart turned and grinned. "I suppose this is where I should say something like, 'make your daddy proud'...but—"

They both laughed. Then a somber moment passed.

"Since you haven't asked me," Coralina blurted, "and I have no idea why, I guess I'll jump in with both feet before what has been hanging in the air dissipates into something both of us wish we'd spoken of." Her white skinned fingers reached out for his hand. It was warm and comforting. "I want you to stand by my side, Rampart. Will you join me on the throne?"

Her question sliced the air and left the ringing bell a distant distraction.

Rampart froze, his hand still joined with hers. This was not the reason for her decision to make Ozil and Mabyn head guard instead of him explanation he was expecting. Rampart withdrew his hand. He had grown to love and respect Coralina over the last year. All they had been through together sent memories racing through his mind. His chest rose and fell twice before he looked directly into the many facets of Coralina's crystal blue eyes. They sparkled with hope that quickly dulled behind clouds of doubt.

"Are you asking me to be the Capitan of your Guard or your bed, Coralina?

"Both. I'm asking you to join with me, Rampart, to rule Faery Lands beside me as my mate." Coralina's mouth spread in a smile that did not include her hopeful eyes. "Together we would make our world strong and safe..." she lowered her eyes and blushed, "and as romantically enchanting as it should be."

Rampart turned his eyes up to the arrow slit and the town he knew was outside the castle grounds. "I am not a king, nor would I make a good ruler of our kingdom, or a father of your ... our children. I like to sleep under the stars not under brick and mortar. I want to fight with the guard, not rule it from a throne. I'm a vagabond, a half breed. And although I love you with all my heart, I'm not suited to sit on a—"

"But I..."

Rampart put his finger over her lips. "I can, and will, protect you and your people until my last breath, but I cannot do it from the throne."

Coralina took his hand from her lips and smiled. "Then we will rule from the guard together. I'll fight by your side, Queen and King together until death takes us."

A deep burbling rose to throaty laughter, and Rampart said, "It's a little late for you to step down and toss your crown to the wind, Cor."

Rampart's laughter made Coralina smile. "And why the hell not? I'll toss the crown to Mabyn while we roam the world and... and do whatever you do as a Queen's guard—"

"—good things for our people?" Rampart shook his head. "We... No. You've already done that. And now it's time to take your rightful place as ruler." Rampart pulled her in front of him and pointed to the arrow slit. "Walk back up there and look down at them coming forth with great hope for a much better future," he said, his left hand on her shoulder. "They are who you belong to, and always have. Not me. Neither of us could possibly do each other's calling while joined together." He gently touched her cheek and turned her face to him. Her eyes were pools of crystal clear water atop a pool of blue. He put his hands on both of her shoulders and smiled when she put hers around his waist. "You can do this. I will be proud to serve you, My Lady, not impregnant you."

Rampart laughed when Coralina shoved him away and threw her hands in the air.

"Fine," she spat. "Now I must look for a man good enough for the seat. One that thinks like me and is not simply courting me to be king..." She glared at him. "...over me. One that will stir up desire and lusty thoughts in my bed."

Rampart's eyelids attempted to shade his jealousy.

"What?" Coralina asked. "You know I will be expected to have a family. And if I refuse to choose someone, someone I do not love, I will be miserable the rest of my life. I love you, damn it! You! I can never love—"

"Crap," Rampart said. His mind raged at the thought of someone else in her bed. Someone else fathering her children. Someone else... "Someone else," he said, and pulled her close.

Coralina held him tight. "Yes, someone else."

"Now what the name of all that is hell do the two of you think you are going to do ten minutes before the crowning?" The words were filled with Hellhound amusement. "Although I have waited to witness your true feelings for each other, this is definitely not the time."

Rampart's lips moved closer to hers and then the laughter from Dusk faded as a fire inside the half-elf rose, one he'd never felt before. One he could not quell alone this time.

While Rampart's lips found her neck, Coralina turned to Dusk. "Shut up, hound. I just proposed, and I believe that kiss was a yes."

Dusk's tail did double time while his body jumped and twisted. "Woohoo! That makes me the Royal—"

"Pain in the ass," Coralina said, and they both looked at Dusk.

"I'm up for that," Dusk said. "Now let's get dressed and get you both crowned." Dusk sat on his rump and lifted his front paws. "Group hug?"